For Diane

MARGARITO AND ME

DAVID KYEA

MARGARITO AND ME

Copyright © 2021 by David Kyea. All rights reserved.

No part of this publication may be translated, reproduced or transmitted in any form or by any means, in whole or in part without prior written permission from the author.

All names and situations represented in this publication are fictitious except those locations used and known to be real. Any resemblance to real people or real situations is unintentional and coincidental.

ISBN: 978-1-09837-263-7
ISBN eBook: 978-1-09837-264-4

Published and Printed in the United States of America by BookBaby
Cover Photo by Jean Nichols: life-long advocate of the arts and community

DEDICATION

I would like to share my appreciation for the four most important women in my life. Without them I would not be and it is to them that I dedicate this volume.

My wife, Lani. Without her encouragement and assistance this volume would most likely never have been written, and certainly never published. It has been her vision that guided me through the highs and lows of adult life and it was she who had the audacity to think that I might actually write something of value. For all the nights you spent sleeping, secure in thethe knowledge that I was across the room, pecking away at the keyboard, and would have produced something for you to read in the morning . . . my heartfelt gratitude.

My mother. It was her early influence that made a reader of me. I am fortunate to have childhood memories of my mother reading with me and my siblings. She always encouraged us and never chided us for our mistakes. It was due to her influence that I received my education, curiosity, freedom, and desire to learn. My sole regret is that she is not here to see what she produced.

My grandmothers. One gave birth to two, the other to eleven. They were very different people on very different journeys. Yet, they each were, in many ways, complements to each other in my early years. My grandmother in these stories is a person given form by my heart. She could only be a woman at whom my narrator, Ricardo, would never stay angry, whose instruction and advice he would rely on, and who provides not only a home but the tangible and unconditional love that IS, between a grandmother and her grandson.

AUTHOR'S NOTES

I first arrived in New Mexico in the early 1970s and much like my narrator, Ricardo, with one step I entered a world much different from what I had known. Ricardo had the advantages of being here once before as a child, and family whom he hoped would greet him. I knew one person. But as Margarito might say, "that is another story."

Like Ricardo, I had a great many lessons to learn. I found it best to listen, observe, accept, and try things for myself. After all, I was a stranger in someone else's land.

Language was, and remains to me, one of the most wondrous aspects of New Mexico. Many of the elder people I have known spoke Spanish, English, and portions of one or more Native American dialects. New Mexico has historically been home, at least in recent memory, to Navajo, Apache, Ute, Spanish, English, and a variety of Puebloan languages.

I have refrained from overusing many of the unique peculiarities of New Mexico language in my writing at the risk of being less colorful and in the hope of being less tedious to those who are unfamiliar with them. For these reasons I have included a Glossary, such as it is, of New Mexican terms. Words such as "coke" are used in some regions of the state to designate any flavor or brand of soft drink. In parts of New Mexico, a person gets "on" or "off" or "down from" a car or truck.

Sheep in Spanish is borrego, if the speaker is referring to a single animal. In English, sheep is both singular and plural. In Spanish the plural is borregos. In translation, when an old-time Spanish speaker is referring to multiple animals in English, they quite naturally become sheeps. Multiple elk become elks. The simple logic of it has always astounded and pleased me.

I attempted to arrange the stories of this collection in a rough chronological order, something that is difficult for me. I have known persons who can relate the exact date of the big rain in 1923, or the birthdates of their ten siblings, their parents and grandparents, the year the grass was taller than a Thoroughbred's belly, or the summer it was so dry fish had to walk from one water hole to another.

My memory just doesn't work that way. I don't even recall the exact year that I became a resident of New Mexico. It is but one of the spells that have overtaken me since finding my way to the Land of Enchantment(s). Those spells have only increased their hold through years of living by the cycles of sun, moon, stars, and seasons. That, I believe, is the best sort of magic. The stuff of life that doesn't shout out its own wonder at the time but later, sometimes many years later, you realize that its influence has been there, within you, all along.

What I can tell you for certain is that my wife and I have been at home here from the first day of our arrival. We have met a level of acceptance that has been astounding and wonderfully warm. We may not have been born in New Mexico but we have shed enough blood, sweat, and tears on her soil that we might, at least, be considered a small part of her.

The characters in this book are of necessity, fictionalized and at times embellished, impressions of people I have known, worked beside, eaten with, shared good times and not-so-good times with, shared tales with—and learned from. There is always something new to learn. I can only hope that I have left something of value with each person I have known.

The tales in this volume are based in actual experiences, observations, stories that I have heard, or ideas that came to me while nailing tin on a barn roof, fixing a barbed-wire fence, shearing sheep, feeding cattle, playing my guitar or violin, or otherwise going about the everyday business of life.

I know that readers will have varying impressions of my experiences and cultural knowledge. Or lack thereof. That is fine. It is the beauty and wonder of who we are.

The names of towns, mountains, and rivers are also fictional except, of course, those the reader might recognize "for reals."

This volume has been years in the making and I have spent many more years struggling with myself to eventually reach the decision to publish. It has been a herculean effort for my wife to keep me on the path (I am easily distracted) and convince me that I should lift the barrel under which I have kept these stories for so long. I have to agree with her when she says, "You gave them life. Now, it is your duty to let them live on their own merits. It is only fair to them."

My greatest and most earnest hope is that you, the reader, might experience through these tales at least a small portion of the wonder, joy, sorrow, and magic that I enjoyed in writing these stories of humble, yet in their own way exceptional, people and experiences.

A FEW WHO HELPED ME ALONG THE WAY

I must thank the people of New Mexico who shared their culture and life with Lani and me. There have been so many that to thank each of you personally would be a volume much larger than this. And the number continues to grow.

I cannot help but have in mind as I write those we have known that are no longer with us in body. I hope I have done justice through my writing to the knowledge you shared.

Thanks to all who purchased and read my first book, *KITE and Other Short Stories of New Mexico*. Your feedback and kind comments have been uplifting and beyond encouraging.

Special thanks to Tom and Kay Decker who plowed their way through a rough manuscript and replied with pages of suggestions, recommendations, insights, and praise.

I also want to thank my cousin John F. Green and my friend Carmen Baca. They are both prolific writers and published authors who have had faith in my tales and spent a lot of their time urging me to continue and, in the end, publish.

CONTENTS

ME—1

MARGARITO MONTOYA—11

MY TELEPHONE—25

MARGARITO AND SOLO VINO—41

BLACKSMITHS—57

MAYBELLE—69

TÍO MELECIO—97

FLORIAN CISNEROS—111

SHEEP AND SAINTS—127

SOLO VINO—147

TÍA CARMELA—155

TWO ONESIMOS—161

ANTS IN A JAR—179

LA SEPOLTURA—199

GLOSSARY OF TERMS AND WORD USES IN NEW MEXICO—215

ABOUT THE AUTHOR—225

ME

ABOUT A MONTH AFTER MY MOTHER'S STRUGGLE with cancer came to an end, I walked away from college. I'd hung in as long as I could because I hadn't wanted to disappoint her. A week later, during lunch break, I walked out of my part-time job in a Northeastern factory, leaving a half-eaten bologna sandwich on the cafeteria table. I just wasn't looking forward to a life of eight to five, five days a week, mowing a lawn, two weeks a year vacation, drinking beer and watching sports on the weekend. What was worse, I didn't have any idea what I was looking forward to. I just knew that whatever it might be, it wasn't going to happen where I was.

I went home, packed a few clothes, some freeze-dried food, and an army surplus sleeping bag into a fifty-dollar Kelty backpack, left a note on the kitchen table for my father, stuck out my thumb and headed West with my life savings of $363 tucked in a boot. I left behind my father, two married sisters who had taken in my younger sister and baby brother, and a handful of friends.

With no idea why, or what to expect, I headed to the only place I could think of. New Mexico and my mother's family, which I barely knew. Six days later I'd crossed two thirds of the country and found myself trudging along the shoulder of a narrow two-lane highway through the Sangre de Cristo mountains.

I slogged the last six miles to the town of Río Pueblo through a late August downpour, climbing from the Río Grande, over the pass, and down into the valley of the Río del Indio. According to my map, another three miles would get me to my destination of Llano Alto.

Somewhere in the storm-shrouded mountains surrounding the valley, my father, a forest ranger from Vermont, had first seen my mother. She'd been a slender, dark-eyed, black-haired girl of seventeen on horseback, riding alongside her father and brothers as they drove their white-faced cattle to summer pasture.

Dad had two strikes against him from the start. To my future uncles, he was a gringo. Worse, he worked for the forest service, an agency of the government that, a hundred years earlier, had seized the commonly held merced from the Spanish. Resentments die hard where today is no more than a night's sleep away from a past century. My father had been persistent and eventually reached a status with my mother's family that put him on a footing slightly above the family dog. Finally, they let him court her in the hope that she would see the errors of his ways. My sisters, brother, and I were living proof that the idea backfired.

By the time I made it to the town of Río Pueblo the storm had taken a break. A crew of men was breaking down carnival rides in a field behind a tiny restaurant adorned with a hand-lettered sign that read "Roberto's Café." Rain-drenched tissue paper pom-poms and streamers floated by on muddy water running six inches deep in ditches alongside the road. Almost no one was out, except for the line of pickups at Bennie's Package Liquors.

Two of the three family-owned general stores, the two restaurants, and a lone auto parts store were all closed. One gas station was still open. I waved to the people standing inside. They watched from behind a plate glass window as I trudged past. A kid in a red plaid shirt waved back. It was getting late.

I hurried up the road out of the valley toward Llano Alto. I remembered this road as unpaved. At least I wasn't struggling my way uphill through six inches of mud. The downpour let loose again, doing its best to drown me. Water ran in streams from my drooping felt hat and leaked through seams in the cheap plastic poncho I'd bought three days before in Joplin.

The pavement ended at the Llano Alto plaza. With one stride, I stepped from mainstream 1970s America into that world which had been restlessly slumbering within me for over a decade. It was nearly sunset when I arrived at my grandmother's and pushed through the gate into her yard. I just stood there.

Memories competed with rain for my attention. I hadn't been here since I was ten; twelve years ago, and the only time as a family we had been to New Mexico. My cousins had teased me mercilessly and given their half-breed coyote kin a fat lip and black eye. I spent the next week following in the safety of my grandfather's boot prints around the family farm. He patiently demonstrated for me the basics of gardening, pruning fruit trees, chopping firewood, irrigating fields, sharpening tools, and caring for livestock. The rich odors of earth, water, animals, wood smoke, and mountain air were intoxicants that have never been purged from my soul.

I hadn't wondered where my parents were or what they were doing while I followed his denim-jacketed shoulders, shaded beneath a beat up wide-brimmed black hat. I never had to seek his approval. His smile was enough. It seems now that I'd been infected by this man who left footprints not only in the earth, but on my spirit.

And there was the night my grandfather came unannounced to my bedroom in Vermont. It had been three years since I'd seen him. My parents must have been keeping his visit a secret.

I don't know what it was that woke me but there he was, standing at the foot of my bed. I sat up and softly called out to him, "Granpo?"

He lifted his hat from his head. I remember how white his forehead was in contrast to the dark, weathered tan of his lined face and coal-black hair. Clothes rustled softly as he slowly approached my side. Except for the cowlick that jutted up from the back of his head, his hair was neatly combed. He stood there smiling, in a faded and patched denim jacket, hat held gently before him in dark work-strong hands. I settled back onto my pillow. He leaned over me, lifted the blankets around my shoulders and laid his hand lightly on my head. The scents of earth and mountains were strong. I fell back to sleep looking forward to morning and the opportunity to show him my new bicycle.

It was still dark when the phone rang. My mother answered. Silence. She started to cry. I jumped from bed and ran to the kitchen. My father, phone to his ear, held my mother in his arms. Somehow, I knew. My grandfather was dead. That morning was the first big disappointment of my life. The one against which I have measured all others, and found them lacking.

The memory of that morning spurred me toward the house, his house, and my grandmother. Wisps of fragrant blue smoke struggled skyward from a precariously angled stovepipe and disappeared into the rain above the roof, promising warmth and dry clothes. The mud in the yard was slick. I slipped and fell. The stuff stuck to my clothes and hands in thick globs that even the downpour couldn't wash clean. Two shepherd-mix dogs growled from the shelter of a nearby low-roofed log barn. Their suspicious, bloodshot eyes followed every step I took.

A handful of miserable-looking sheep huddled nervously behind the dogs, in the back of the barn. One that I took for a ram stamped his feet and glared at me.

I knew I didn't look too good and was faintly worried about what kind of reception I might receive. I hadn't called. I didn't know the phone number or even if my grandmother had a phone. No one answered my knock. I tried the door. It wasn't locked but I didn't go in.

Beneath the porch, I slid the backpack from my shoulders, leaned it against a neat stack of split firewood, and tugged a cheap wool blanket from it. Wrapping the blanket around me, I settled down on the worn boards of the porch. With my back against the blue-painted adobe wall, I sat. And waited.

It struck me how little I knew about my mother and her life as a child or why she never taught me to speak Spanish. It hadn't been something she or my father talked about. Now, thinking about it . . . it seemed that once she and my father left New Mexico, they just closed the book. They never spoke harshly or negatively about her home or family, they just hardly ever mentioned them at all. I guess that sometimes making a living can get in the way of life. Or maybe it was more like, "That was then, this is now." Or, maybe, if she had started sharing memories with me, she would have wanted to return.

Rain beat steadily on the tin roof and splashed noisily into the clean-swept dirt yard. The water made little brown foamy rivulets that wandered off toward the Río Pequeño. Bass-throated thunder rolled along the sides of cloud-shrouded mountains, leaping from peak to peak. The valley shuddered.

I shivered and pulled my wet muddy legs under the blanket. Serenaded by thunder, the beat of rain, and an occasional half-hearted yip from the outraged dogs, I fell asleep. My last thought was, "I sure hope this is the right house."

I woke to headlights in my eyes and rapid-fire shouted Spanish. I didn't understand a word. It had stopped raining, mostly. Night had arrived while I slept. The dogs, who had been snuffling around my feet, jumped back stiff-legged, growling menacingly. I tried to stand. My legs had gone numb and I had to lean against the wall to keep my balance. The dogs took another step back and started barking. I rubbed my eyes with muddy fingers and tried to see through the glare of the headlights. Silhouettes splashed busily in the rain-drenched yard. A car door slammed shut.

A tiny walnut-skinned woman, in a bright blue plastic raincoat and matching floppy- brimmed hat, appeared suddenly beside me. It was her. My grandmother. She looked up, nodding slowly. In the bend of her left arm she held a rain-spotted brown paper sack with celery sticking out the top. A woman shouted from somewhere behind the headlights. The strength of the old woman's voice beside me as she shouted back in Spanish caused me to jump.

She turned and just stood there, for what seemed a minute, appraising me. I must have looked like a castoff mud-caked puppy that had sought refuge on her porch. I shivered. Finally, she turned and waived emphatically to whoever was in the car. The headlights slowly backed out of the yard.

"Come in where it's warm, Ricardito. And take off those wet muddy clothes."

It was that simple. I never asked how she knew it was me on her porch that day. It was just never that important.

I washed most of the mud off in a white enamel bowl before she showed me to a bedroom where I could change. Urged along by the smells of fresh coffee, beans, and tortillas I'd barely gotten into dry clothes when the house was besieged by visitors. Headlights swept through the rain and trees around the house as vehicles made the turn off the llano road and slid into the muddy yard. Feet stamped on the boards of the porch. Raised voices boiled out from the kitchen. The dogs barked. I didn't understand much of what was being said, most of it was in Spanish, but the tone was definitely incredulous. And angry. It seemed that at least fifteen people had stormed the house, each shouting louder than the others.

My father once told me how my uncles threatened to kill him for his attention to my mother. He'd laughed about it then, but it had made an impression on me. I wasn't about to become the victim of twenty-four years' unsatisfied vengeance and decided to stay in the bedroom, hoping to avoid a confrontation. I looked around the room and waited for the commotion to settle.

The walls were a glossy lime green. Inexpensive cream and pink floral print linoleum covered the floor. There was no closet. Religious prints wrapped in plastic hung on a wall: Pope John Paul, Our Lady of Guadalupe, St. Joseph holding the curly-headed child Jesus and a staff festooned with hollyhocks. What I took for a Roman soldier leaned from a horse, cutting his red cloak with a sword. A grateful beggar beamed up at the horseman from a pile of rocks and rags on the ground. The name beneath them read "San Martín Caballero." Below the pictures, on a handmade glossy varnished and elaborately carved pine chest were a Bible, a plastic crucifix draped with a red rosary, photographs, and a lit votive candle. The flame flickered reassuringly.

On the adjacent wall were photographs of my mother, father, and what I assumed were aunts, uncles, in-laws, cousins, and one of myself when I was about six years old, dressed for Easter. In the photo I was wearing plaid pants and vest over a white shirt and a red bow tie.

The cowlick that still plagued me was standing straight up on the back of my head. My mother and my father, holding my oldest sister in his arms, flanked me on either side.

A large sepia-toned portrait of a bearded man, intense blue eyes in a deeply lined face, hung in an oval fake-tortoiseshell frame. He had an uncontrolled cowlick too. I wasn't sure but I thought he might be my great grandfather. My grandfather and I had been named for him.

The room obviously wasn't getting a lot of use. Except for my wet, muddy clothes that I'd shed in a pile next to the door, it was spotlessly clean. A few cardboard boxes were neatly arranged along one wall and an inexpensive dime-store lamp with a plastic floral shade sat on a carved pine nightstand, casting a warm yellow sixty-watt glow. The bed was covered with a gloriously colored homemade quilt. I knew this room, just as it was, even though it had been twelve years since I had set foot in this house. God, I was tired.

The voices radiating from the kitchen had gradually quieted down. They actually sounded calm, soothing. I lay back on the bed. My head sank deep into a down pillow. I let my eyes wander idly over the vigas and latillas of the ceiling, searching the shadows and patterns in the wood for familiar faces and animals, remembered from my childhood. I slept deep. And I dreamed . . .

A bearded man with a cowlick slept on a homemade quilt. A tiny gray-haired woman in a long black dress and blue plastic boots covered him with a thick, woolen, striped blanket.

A young man, scarred, battered, and emaciated, wandered through the house. He stopped and stood before a fragment of mirror. The house was different. There was no paint, no porch, and the walls were finished with a simple cream colored, earth plaster. The roof was flat. A demon fled, shrieking, from a grave.

Behind me a guitar struck up a slow waltz. Then, a violin. I turned and came face to face with a big yellow-eyed, shaggy gray dog. The dog became a man. The man blinked in surprise and smiled.

Alabados floated on the morning air and a black cow, all skin and bones, wandered in snow to her belly. The struggle for life burned feverishly, deep in her eyes. I reached for her. She turned away.

Thunder rolled along cloud-shrouded ridges and rumbled in the earth. Generations passed silently through the lime green room and I wondered how in the world I would ever get the floor clean.

MARGARITO MONTOYA

It was my uncle Freddie who told me why everyone had been so upset when I arrived in Llano Alto. He showed up at my grandmother's house the morning after I got there. My grandmother was at the woodstove cooking a breakfast of eggs, fried potatoes, green chiles, and bacon when Freddie's dented, bullet-hole riddled, misfiring and broken-windowed pickup pulled into the yard. I was sitting at the kitchen table answering questions as they occurred to my grandmother, about my mother, father, sisters, and brother.

Freddie slammed the door to his truck.

I looked out the window.

"Who's that?" I asked my grandmother's back.

"Your tío Freddie."

She hadn't even turned to look.

Freddie swung open the door and strode into the kitchen. He barely glanced at me, went straight to my grandmother and wrapped his arms around her. He kissed her hair and gave her neck a nibble. She giggled and pushed him away with her elbow. He poured himself a cup of coffee and sat at the table, across from me.

"Sooooo, this is the long-lost grandson. Or in my case, sobrino. Ricardito. You've grown a bit since the last time I saw you. But not so much as the others led me to believe. The way they told it last night, you were some sort of giant red-eyed beast with the fangs and claws of a lion. A born-again devil, come to steal their mother's farm and their one-fiftieth of inheritance. You aren't, are you?"

"Huh?"

"That's what I thought. Don't worry. They were just mad because the fiestas got rained out and were too drunk to see straight."

"Fiestas?"

"They should have known better. Weren't we all raised under the same roof? The real beast is there" . . . he pointed with his lips to my grandmother . . . "at the stove."

I threw a hurried glance toward her.

She snorted "hah," turned, and shook an eight-inch knife at her son. She was smiling.

"If it hadn't been for her and her wood spoon . . . the same one we all learned to dread when we were children, who knows what might have happened?"

"Uuuuh . . ." I'd been reduced to monosyllables by his chatter. But it didn't slow him down. Not a bit.

"She stood there, with her back to the door of the room where you were hiding, and fended them off. If it hadn't been for her and your tío Solomon, Carolina's husband, ¿quién sabe?" He shrugged his shoulders. "I only wish I'd been here to see it."

"I wasn't hiding."

"Sooo, you do know how to talk." He looked intently at me, evaluating what to say next.

"Well then, if you weren't hiding, you should have been. My brothers and their wives are the meanest people in all the mountains." He winked. "Except, now they live in Santa Fe and Albuquerque."

My grandmother jumped into it then. "Freddie. Stop it! You know that's not true."

She turned from the stove and carried two plates, heaping with food, to the table and set one in front of each of us.

"What's not true? That they live in Albuquerque? Or Santa Fe?" She whapped him with a fist on top of his head.

"Where's yours, Grandma?" I asked.

"I ate while you were sleeping." She went back to the stove, returned with the coffeepot, and filled our cups. Freddie jumped up as she started back to the stove and took the pot from her hand. "Mama. Sit," he gently insisted.

Freddie and I dug into our breakfast. Grandma sipped her coffee, watching with satisfaction. Between mouthfuls, Freddie caught up on how I'd traveled across the country, told me where he lived, discussed his wife Helen's health, the condition of my grandmother's sheep, and asked whether or not I knew how to split firewood, shear sheep, prune trees, cut and bale hay, dig a ditch, irrigate a field, fix a barbed-wire fence, nail tin to a roof, saddle a horse, brand cattle . . . The list was overwhelming and I have to admit, by the time he ran through it all, I was feeling pretty useless.

Despite his never-ending one-sided conversation, Freddie finished eating first and pushed his plate to the center of the table. He watched me over the rim of his cup as he downed the last of his coffee.

When he was done, he stood. "Well, I have to get to work at Lebanon's. He has a plugged drain in the store and hired me to clear it for him."

He bent over, gave my grandmother a peck on the cheek and started to the door. Halfway there he stopped and turned. "I'm glad that you have come home, Ricardo. The others will be too, once they realize that you are not here to steal something from them. Where will you be staying?"

To tell the truth I hadn't thought that far ahead. Before I could answer, my grandmother spoke up. "He will be living here. With me."

Freddie grinned. "Good. He has a lot to learn and there is no better teacher. Later."

With that, he was out the door and gone.

One of the daily tasks that my grandmother had me do for her was walk to the Llano Alto Post Office and pick up the mail. It didn't make a whole lot of sense to me at first. I could have gone every few days and come home with an armful but she insisted that I make the trip every day, except Sundays and certain holidays when the post office was closed. It took a while for me to realize that my grandmother was the only person I knew who had a fondness for junk mail.

In the course of a month I would lug home a foot and a half tall stack of catalogs for racy lingerie; book club offerings for best sellers or the classics, all in English which she could barely read; catalogs for appliances she neither wanted, needed, knew how to use, or could afford; and ads for garden tools and supplies that she would never use and plants that would never grow in our high mountain valley. She never bought any of it. None. Ever. Two or three times a month she would receive a letter from a friend or someone in the family living in Albuquerque, Nevada, Colorado, California, or Santa Fe.

One day a week, usually a Thursday, she would just sit at the kitchen table for hours, a stack of catalogs beside her, smiling, singing softly to herself, intently studying the pictures, flipping from page to page and back again, a pair of red plastic-handled scissors in her wrinkled brown hand. She'd clip pictures from flyers, catalogs, or brochures and carefully paste them into cheap spiral notebooks. There were boxes overflowing with the things in her room.

Once, when she was out of town with my tía Carolina, curiosity got the best of me and I looked through one of the notebooks. On one glue-wrinkled page there was a picture of a refrigerator next to a well-endowed blonde in a bikini. Another wrinkly page held a picture of a basket full of puppies; another, an ad for a seed catalog featuring a huge watermelon held by a sandy-haired kid in a red-and-white striped T-shirt, grinning from ear to ear. The whole book was like that. I came to think of the books as her entertainment. We didn't have a television and the only radio station we could get was from a town seventy miles and two mountain ranges away, famous for top-secret government projects.

The post office was the unofficial social hub of Llano Alto, even more so than the church, which was only occasionally used for a funeral or the annual Mass on the feast day of its patron saint. Most people went to church in nearby Río Pueblo.

There was no residential mail delivery. All incoming mail was dropped off at the "P.O." in a stained and patched, once-white canvas bag with "US MAIL" stenciled on it in faded blue letters, promptly at eleven, by a contract driver in a battered red Chevy pickup. He was usually gone in a cloud of dust, the outgoing mail stuffed into yesterday's canvas bag and tossed in the bed of the truck, within five minutes of his arrival. By eleven twenty each envelope, magazine, catalog, ad, sales flyer, or notice of a package had been placed by Della, the postmistress, in its appropriate box.

I hadn't been able to locate a paying job and the walk to the post office was a break in the daily chores of pruning trees; splitting firewood; irrigating the orchard, garden, and sheep pasture; painting the kitchen a very bright yellow that nearly blinded me; splitting more firewood; replacing boards on the porch; nailing down loose sheets of tin roofing; fixing fences; sweeping the yard around the house; splitting even more firewood; feeding sheep; or weeding the garden. I usually managed to take up most of forty-five minutes on the round trip.

I'd devised a route that switchbacked up the side of the llano, across an ancient overgrown trash heap, between two houses, past the old school which had been abandoned since the late 1950s and out into the Llano Alto plaza. One of the houses on my route was empty and looked like it had been for quite a while. The other, according to local gossip, had recently been bought by a family from Albuquerque.

On one of my trips I saw the Albuquerque people out front raking the yard. I walked over to introduce myself. They saw me coming and scurried into the house. I knocked on the screen door they had just disappeared through. No one answered. Llano Alto had that effect sometimes on outsiders.

The trash heap was mostly overgrown by some kind of spindly grass that never seemed to be green and various sticker-bearing weeds. It was no longer used and I probably wouldn't even have known it was there except, one day, the maintainer driver for the county road department happened to cut deep into the side of the llano, revealing layers of centuries-old debris and knocking more rocks onto the road than he removed.

Historically, nobody in Llano Alto throws anything away that has the least redeeming quality or slightest vestige of utility. Mostly, the trash heap was layer on layer of ashes from woodstoves and an occasional ancient animal bone that had, for reasons of its own, protruded into the daylight. Once in a while, a twisted piece of rusty barbed wire, scabrous iron, bent fork or spoon, broken crockery, the bottom half of an enameled coffee pot, rusty bed spring, a handle from one device or another, or the fragile rust-riddled remnants of a tin can would struggle from its ashy grave to the surface.

Most of the risen artifacts were beyond redemption, but I managed to retrieve four mostly intact arrowheads and numerous pieces of flint that led me to believe the dump predated Spanish occupation, a dozen or so pieces of pottery of various ages and designs, a handful of glass beads, most of a rosary, and a Civil War–era military belt buckle. An antique dealer in La Plaza offered me five dollars for the buckle. I decided to keep it.

On any given day, at least one representative from each family in Llano Alto made their way to the post office to exchange gossip and pick up mail. The post office, which also served as a more or less general store, was in the end room of a long thick-walled adobe that made up half of one side of the plaza. The remaining half dozen rooms of the house were occupied by Della, her husband Carlos, and at least four kids.

The post office/general store had a high, pressed-tin ceiling and hardwood floors. The tin ceiling was an extravagance from bygone days designed to impress customers, and hardwood floors were a true rarity in Llano Alto. Most people either spread inexpensive floral-patterned linoleum over hard-packed dirt or nailed rough-sawn pine boards from one of the local sawmills over two-by-four stringers. In the old days, before linoleum and sawmills, according to my grandmother, the dirt floors had been treated with ox blood which made a durable, deep red/brown surface.

Along the wall to the right, as you entered, Della kept long shelves, behind a longer counter, stocked with a few staples like plastic bags of chicos, powdered red chile, coarse-ground red chile, ten-pound burlap sacks of pinto beans, cans of Wolf brand chili, assorted candy, bags of salt, flour, and sugar, a dozen yellow cans of Rosco dog food, jars of instant coffee, and Spam.

Bolts of sun-faded yellow, red, and blue calico on the top shelf were mute reminders of more prosperous times. At the back of the room, a chipped white enamel cooler wheezed and rattled. The cooler held a random and ever-varying mixture of bottled cokes at just less than room temperature that Della sold for fifteen cents each.

In winter, a pleasant dry heat issued from a massive, round cast-iron stove in the center of the room. In summer, the thick-walled adobe building was a welcome retreat from the heat. If you arrived before eleven you were usually greeted by a crowd of six to a dozen people who generally stood around gossiping until the mail had been pigeonholed in the rack of open-backed wooden mail boxes at the end of the counter near the door. Each box had a little number hand- painted beneath it from one to fifty. My grandmother's mail box was number eight, which meant she held a certain status in the community reserved for those people having one of the lowest-numbered, earliest-issued boxes.

Whenever I walked into the P.O. everybody would go silent. I took it sort of personal at first, until my grandmother explained that it was just the way things were done. Nobody really knew me and I didn't speak Spanish. It was just peoples' way of being polite. If I wanted to enter the conversation, I could. If I didn't want to, I wasn't obligated to. Nobody meant me any ill will and since I didn't speak Spanish, I wouldn't have been able to contribute much anyway.

There was a day when I hadn't been able to find anything that caught my attention in the trash heap. The pickings had been getting progressively slimmer and I suspected that the Albuquerque kids were pilfering my find. A good rain would wash a few treasures back to the surface. I arrived at the post office a little early.

Three or four dusty pickups with rifles in racks in the rear windows, one with an attached beat-up stock trailer containing a saddled horse, were parked in the plaza in a ragged attempt at order. The horse shifted his weight as I passed. Hooves made a hollow thump in the trailer.

As usual, silence blanketed the room as soon as the screen door closed behind me. I nodded to a couple men that I more or less recognized as regulars and slid past the knot of people to the cooler at the back of the room. I chose a bright red coke, the kind that tastes like bubble gum and turns your tongue and lips red, dropped two dimes into the jar at the end of the counter, slid back the way I had come and positioned myself out of the way by the storefront windows.

Della leaned on the counter, smiled, and waved discreetly at me. I smiled back and turned my attention to three ratty-looking dogs wandering the dust of the plaza. They were busy sniffing and baptizing truck tires.

The conversation resumed behind me with an occasional Spanglish word thrown in for emphasis or when there wasn't a Spanish word that quite fit. A few flies buzzed loudly against the screen door. The summer morning chill was fading. It was going to be hot this afternoon.

Suddenly, the dogs scurried out of the path of a big gray car that sped into the plaza. The car slid around the corner and out of sight, leaving behind a haze of dust that drifted lazily over the parked pick-ups, toward the church. The dogs headed eagerly in the direction of the corner where the car had disappeared. I figured the driver must have parked, and shifted my attention to a cloud in the sky that looked like a rabbit with two tails. It was undergoing a slow metamorphosis and I was curious to see what it would become next. Car doors thumped closed. The dogs yipped and ran back into the plaza.

All heads turned as the P.O. door swung open and in strode two very tall, very blond, athletic looking men in dark suits, white shirts, and skinny dark ties. Their black wing-tip shoes were so highly polished that the ankle-deep dust of the plaza hadn't stuck to them. The creases in their pants were knife-blade sharp. They strode purposefully to the counter. Della lost her smile. The chatter of gossip stopped. Feet shuffled. Hands went into pockets. The dogs ran back around the corner, behind the post office.

One of the blond men mumbled and removed something from inside his suit coat that he showed briefly to Della. Her expression didn't change. The other man stood with his back to the counter and faced the rest of us.

"We're looking for José Trujillo." He pronounced it "Joe Say Troo Jillow," with an emphasis on the Joe and the Troo. "Does anyone here know him?" He was loud, with a drawly accent. Blank looks all around.

"We have reason to believe that he lives here in Llano Alto." He pronounced it "Lan no Al toe."

A dozen dark heads shook slowly, negatively. A few denim or flannel clad shoulders shrugged. José Trujillo shrugged and looked blankly at the man next to him. The man next to him just looked back and shrugged. I turned to the rabbit in the sky. Now it was a duck. One of the tails had detached itself and looked like a freshly laid egg.

Della told the men, in a heavy accent that I hadn't heard her use before, that there was no mailbox for José Trujillo. It probably wasn't a lie. Most of the post office boxes in Llano Alto were used by brothers, sisters, in-laws, nieces, nephews, cousins, various extended family members whether or not they still lived in the valley, and an occasional friend of the family. A box might be on file in the name of any one of them. Some boxes, still in the names of departed family members, were lasting memorials to the first person in the clan to receive mail. It was a wonder how Della never got the mail mixed up and always seemed to know whose mail went into which box.

The two men in suits just looked at each other. One of them started to say something but the other shook his head slightly. They turned together on their heels and retreated out the door, letting it slam behind them. They stood arguing for a moment under the porch. I caught bits of their conversation. ". . . Mexicans don't even understand English . . . no street names or telephones." They stomped into the dust of the plaza toward the corner where the gray car had disappeared earlier.

The dogs yipped and ran around the building, tails between their legs and out into the center of the plaza. They turned and glared back toward the corner. One of them, hackles up, barked in stiff-legged outrage. Car doors slammed and the gray car backed into the plaza, turned and sped away, nearly sideswiping the incoming mail truck. Another haze of dust floated up and over the pickups. Nobody said anything after the men in suits left.

Della handed off the outgoing bag and got busy sorting the newly arrived mail. The red pickup left in a cloud of dust and blue exhaust. We all made a polite, raggedy line while we waited for Della to finish stuffing boxes. I went last. Still, nobody spoke.

Finally, one of the men, a little bright-eyed guy with uncombed black hair and a deeply tanned friendly face said, "Anybody dressed like that, they've got to be FBI, IRS, or Mormon missionaries. And I don't think those guys were missionaries."

His hands waved expressively when he spoke. I instantly liked him.

Everybody laughed and stepped aside to let José Trujillo pick up his mail and leave. The rest of us politely took our turns extracting letters, magazines, and junk mail from the boxes. Everyone politely thanked Della as they sauntered out to the plaza. Most of the junk mail went into a trash can beside the door.

I set the empty coke bottle on the counter so Della could collect the deposit and retrieved my grandmother's catalogs. I folded a lingerie catalog into the middle of the stack where no one would see it and waved goodbye to Della as I left. She smiled back and told me to say hello to my grandmother.

I stepped out into the rising heat and dust of the plaza. A couple of the guys that had been in the post office were leaning against the bed of one of the pickups, talking. They acknowledged me by lifting their heads. I nodded back. The truck with the horse in the trailer was gone. The dogs were wandering off toward the church.

The little guy that had made the IRS, FBI, Mormon missionary comment shuffled slowly along in the dust of the road ahead of me. It looked like he was reading something. I stuffed my grandmother's mail into a jacket pocket and hurried to catch up to him.

He must have heard me coming because he stopped and slowly turned toward me. His eyes sparkled. He smiled. Good-natured creases appeared in his face. He stuck his mail under an arm and held out his hand.

"Margarito Montoya," he offered brightly.

It seemed like I'd met him somewhere before but I couldn't figure where. *A guitar? A violin? A shaggy gray dog?* I shook it off and took his hand in a gentle non-challenging clasp, little more than a polite touch, common to the Spanish people of the Southwest, and introduced myself as Guadalupe Gonzales' grandson, Rick.

He pointed with his lips to my jacket pocket. "I see Guadalupe is still getting her catalogs. Do you have time for a cup of coffee and some bizcochitos? Dulcinia Sanchez makes the best and I just bought a couple dozen from her yesterday."

There was no way I could refuse an offer like that.

MY TELEPHONE

MY GRANDMOTHER WAS A WONDER. She cooked Thanksgiving turkeys, Christmas hams, Easter leg of lamb, red or green chile, heaping pots of beans, bread, cakes, pies, enchiladas, and tortillas... all on her gleaming black and chrome wood cookstove.

She served as midwife to ewes having difficulty with lambing, treated almost any kind of wound in man or beast, and knew what herbs would cure most ailments. On top of that she sewed, knit, hoed weeds in the garden, kept a spotlessly clean house, did laundry in her thirty- year-old wringer washing machine, sheared sheep, preserved fruit from her orchard and veggies from her garden, and chopped wood. The litany of her abilities and accomplishments would make most saints blush.

Her four-room square adobe house was heated with a pot-bellied woodstove. Her only concessions to modern technology were electric lights, a single cold-water pipe that came into the kitchen from the community water supply, an ancient wheezy refrigerator, a ten-dollar radio with an eight-inch tinfoil extension on the antenna and a sixteen-year-old, rusty green, Chevy half-ton pickup that had been my grandfather's. My grandmother never drove, or cared to.

She was fond of cardboard boxes and used them for storing her scrapbooks, used clothes, pieces of fabric, yarn, glass jars, and whatever else would fit. The boxes were stacked four tall and three deep against a wall of my bedroom. If she couldn't use a thing or store it in one of her boxes, she gave it away.

I'd been living with my grandmother for about six months when I decided to get a full-time job.

I wandered up and down the valley to all the businesses and talked to them about hiring me. Nothing.

Everybody was real polite and said they'd call if they could use me for a day or two. The problem was, my grandma didn't have a telephone. She had never had a telephone. If someone needed to get hold of her, they called the post office in Llano Alto and left a message. Somebody, usually me, would deliver the message and I would drive her over to a neighbor's who would dial the number for her and she'd return the call. She usually kept the call brief and left a couple dollars to cover the cost. In most instances she would get off a letter to whoever had called. If it was an emergency, Della, the postmistress, would send one of her kids to the house with the message.

To find out what it would take to get a phone I drove over the mountain to the La Plaza Rural Telephone Co-op. The lady behind the counter was pleasant enough but said she just couldn't authorize a hook-up order without a thirty-seven-dollar security deposit, a year's co-op membership dues, a hook-up fee, and a damage deposit on the telephone. Plus taxes. She apologized that it was so expensive but since neither my grandmother, nor I, had ever had a phone we were considered "high risk" customers.

She took all my information, told me that they would have to wait three days for my check to clear the bank, unless I paid in cash, and said that they would call to make an appointment to hook up a line. I wondered how she could call me, especially since I was sure I'd told her I didn't have a phone, but I let it go. Maybe the phone company was capable of things I didn't understand.

It didn't matter anyway. I had six dollars and seventy-six cents in my pocket, no checking account, and I needed to buy a couple dollars of gas to get home and drive around looking for a job. I told her I'd have to discuss the matter with my grandmother. She put the form with all my information on it in a scuffed cardboard file box.

I was getting pretty desperate for work and for the next couple weeks went door-to-door to most of our neighbors, making a pest of myself. It wasn't that there wasn't work, it was just that nobody had any money to pay me.

I helped Ralph Espinoza repair his corral gate in exchange for lunch and a matching pair of orange and green pot holders knit by his wife; split two cords of wood for Dulcinia Trujillo and came home with a brown paper shopping sack full of bizcochitos; set about three dozen cedar fence posts for Juan de Dios Sanchez that earned me three days' lunches and a beat-up single-shot .22 rifle that needed a firing pin; and spent most of two days putting a corrugated tin roof on a shed for Bennie Maestas.

Bennie paid me ten bucks that I used to buy a tank of gas and a quart of oil for the truck that I burned up driving around Río Pueblo looking for work. I hung the .22 over my bed until I could get an extra five bucks for a new firing pin, and gave the potholders to my grandmother.

It was maybe my third stop at Lebanon's store when he took pity on me. He offered to pay me fifteen bucks a day, lunch, and gas money to haul off from behind his store a pile of old broken pallets, rotten lumber, busted cinderblocks, corroded and cracked plumbing fixtures, decaying cardboard boxes full of stinking rotten lettuce and tomatoes, exploded cans of vegetables and moldy bread that hadn't sold in the store, half empty buckets of paint, and whatever sorts of things people had been tossing, under cover of darkness, onto the fly-infested eight-foot-tall pile for the past six years. It seemed that Lebanon's wife had finally gotten to the point where she was afraid the whole mess would collapse and bury one or the other, or all, of their kids.

I asked Margarito if he wanted to help but he declined. It seems he had an aversion that I hadn't known about to rats, scorpions, skunks, and snakes, all of which he suspected of inhabiting the trash pile.

"I wouldn't dig in that trash pile unless I had a shotgun with me," he advised. "Who knows what's buried, or living, in there. Or for that matter, who's buried under there."

"I don't have a shotgun, just an old .22 rifle that needs a firing pin." I replied. "What if a snake bites me and I need somebody to drive me to the hospital?"

"You don't have any money to pay the hospital either."

I didn't like where that was going.

It was true that I didn't have any money to pay the hospital or a doctor, which was why I was willing to take the job in the first place. I needed the money so I could get a phone, so I could get a real job and make more money so I could pay the phone bill and do whatever else it was I thought I had to do that required money. Margarito said he'd meet me the next day and buy lunch at Roberto's Café.

The next morning at sunup Lebanon turned me loose with a shovel, a rake, and a warning that he couldn't pay me for more than five days' work and if I hurt myself, he wasn't paying the doctor bills. The way I figured it, that would pay for the phone hook-up, buy a firing pin for the .22 and I'd still have about twenty bucks left over. I wasn't really sure if he was serious about not paying the doctor bills.

I dug in. Shovel after shovel full of all kinds of broken, rotten, and stinking things went into the bed of Grandma's truck. I used some pieces of busted pallets to rig sideboards so I could pile the stuff an extra two feet deep.

At first, I kept my eyes open for anything that might have some redeemable value. After the first truck load it all started looking the same. I gave up hoping to find lost diamond rings or bank bags full of cash and set my mind to getting the job done. At least I didn't run across any snakes, skunks, or scorpions and it seemed like the rats had all run for cover. Probably into the store.

Filling the truck with the junk and garbage wasn't too much trouble. The hard part came after I backed up to the edge of the dump, an open, straight-sided, fifteen-foot-deep pit bulldozed by the county road department into a caliche hilltop. There was just no way I could safely get the stuff out of the truck and into the pit without climbing in it up to my knees and pushing it out the tailgate. Shovelful by shovelful. I got two truckloads hauled off and deposited in the dump that first morning.

I was ready for lunch and headed for Roberto's to meet with Margarito. I drove the five miles back to Río Pueblo with the windows down, trying to blow out some of the dozens of flies that had followed me into the cab.

The funny thing about digging around in garbage is how, after a while, you sort of get used to the smell. I mean, it's still there, but after an hour or two it creeps into your hair, clothes, and pores so the whole world seems to take on the smell and it doesn't gag you anymore. The problem is that other people can smell it, or you, if you've been messing with the stuff.

I got to Roberto's before Margarito, washed my hands and face in the men's room, poured me a cup of coffee at the machine on the counter, and took a seat in one of the booths by the window where I could look out at Sierra Rota. The place was empty. I waved to Roberto and his wife, Lucia, who were in the kitchen preparing for the lunch rush and shouted to them that I was waiting for Margarito. They grinned and nodded.

A young couple showed up and dropped into the booth next to me. They held hands, giggled for a while and waited for Lucia to take their order. After a few minutes they started whispering and looking at me. I smiled and sipped my coffee. They got up and moved a few seats away. I figured they thought I was eavesdropping on them, which I was.

A few minutes later, a handful of schoolteachers drove up and wandered in. I knew some of them and nodded to each as they came through the door. They nodded back and filled a booth, two down from me. Lucia came out and took the order from the young couple. The teachers ordered drinks. Lucia smiled in my direction and went back to the kitchen.

She came back a few minutes later, delivered drinks to the teachers and approached me with the coffeepot in her hand. She asked if I wanted a refill on my coffee. I noticed that she was sniffing and looking around, all inquisitive. I took a refill. She just shook her head and returned to the kitchen.

After a few minutes the teachers quieted down. They started whispering and looking in my direction. I turned and looked behind me, nothing there. I waved and smiled at them. They all got up and moved down to another booth just as Margarito and a handful of cars pulled into the parking lot.

The place filled up. Everybody seemed to be in a pretty good mood and they all waved and chattered away as they placed orders or took seats. Margarito plopped into the seat across from me.

"Sorry I'm late, I almost forgot. What's that smell?" he asked.

"I don't smell anything."

He sniffed the air. "Smells like something rotten. Maybe a skunk."

I guess he said it loud enough for other people to hear because a young girl in her orange and black cheerleader outfit sitting in the booth behind me turned around and said, "I smell it too."

The two men in the booth behind Margarito said they smelled it. They had ordered to go.

The cheerleader told her boyfriend to change places with her. They swapped seats in the booth. A couple minutes later the boyfriend spoke up. "I smell it now. It smells like . . . garbage." They slid out of the booth and left, leaving Lucia standing behind the counter holding two milkshakes in her hands.

I guess she'd seen the kids talking to us, so came over to where Margarito and I were sitting.

"What happened, why did they leave?" she asked.

Margarito told her that something smelled bad in the café and maybe a skunk had gotten under the floor. She sniffed around a little bit and shook her head. "I smell it too. It's over here by this booth. Why don't you move to another one?" We did, toward the schoolteachers.

A few minutes and a lot of whispering later, one of the teachers, I think it was Manuel Sanchez, got up and strode to the counter. He told Lucia that they wanted their orders to go. The other teachers were already headed to the door.

Roberto, wiping his hands on a towel, came out from the kitchen. "Is there a problem?" he asked Manuel. He tried to sound all friendly but it was obvious he was worried.

Manuel told him right out that something in the restaurant smelled rotten. The young couple that had been the first to move said they smelled it too. The two men, two booths down, said that they smelled it, Margarito said he smelled it. Everybody else in the place said they smelled it. I said I didn't smell anything. Lucia said she had smelled it by the booth where Margarito and I had been sitting and she had told us to move.

Roberto came around from behind the counter and walked over to the booth where we had been sitting. It got all quiet and everybody in the place turned to watch him. "I smell it." He pronounced. "But it's faint."

He leaned over toward the two men with the to-go orders and sniffed. "Nothing over here."

He walked over to Margarito and me. "It's stronger over this way." He stopped and looked at me. He leaned toward me and sniffed. He leaned closer and sniffed. He stepped back.

"Jeez Ricardo. What happened? Did you die and forget to bury yourself?"

It dawned on me. My face turned all hot and I got up as quick as I could. "Oh shit Roberto, I'm sorry, I've been cleaning up Lebanon's garbage pile because I need to make enough money for a hook-up fee and security deposit so I can get a telephone so I can get a job and taking the stuff to the dump and I didn't think . . ."

One of the two men that had been sitting next to us earlier, laughed. "I wouldn't go near Lebanon's trash pile without a shotgun."

Margarito just looked down at the table in front of him. He was laughing and shaking his head, all at the same time.

I stood up and headed to the back door of the café as fast as I could.

The short of it was, Margarito ordered and brought out a lunch of red chile enchiladas, which we ate sitting under an apple tree in Roberto's yard next to the café. He told me that everybody in the café had a good laugh. Roberto and Lucia wiped down the seats where I'd been sitting and sprayed some kind of sanitary deodorizer in the café.

After lunch I went back to work on Lebanon's trash pile and hauled off two more loads that afternoon. My grandmother wouldn't let me in the house until I stripped down and hosed off myself and my clothes. I hung the clothes on the line where I could easily get to them in the morning.

The next four days I ate my lunch of cold Vienna sausage, peanut butter cheese crackers, and canned peaches alone, leper-like, on the tailgate of the truck. I finished up a little after noon on the fifth day. Lebanon inspected the job and said he was satisfied. He paid me for the five full days even though I'd finished more or less four hours sooner than he'd calculated.

The next day was Saturday. The phone company was closed. They were closed on Sunday too. I thought that was darned inconsiderate of them.

Monday morning I left the house at first light and made it to the phone company offices before anyone was there to even open the doors. I sat in the truck and waited. Nobody showed up. The warm, late spring, morning sunlight streamed into the truck cab. I fell asleep.

I woke up. Still no people, no cars and no trucks in the parking lot. I couldn't figure it out. The sun looked like it must be close to ten thirty. I got off the truck, walked over to the heavy glass doors in the front of the building and read the magic-markered index card sign taped on the inside, "Closed Monday 4 Morial Day." It looked like whoever wrote the card started out too big and ran out of room to put in "Memorial." "Day" was really tiny and sort of tucked in under "Morial." It took me a couple seconds to decipher the thing. I read it again.

I walked back to the truck. It seemed like a conspiracy. Maybe my grandmother was right not to have things like telephones, televisions, and the like. She seemed about as happy as anyone I knew, maybe even happier than most people. After all, having things just cost money and you had to keep working just to keep paying for more things made by other people so they could get paid so they could buy more things made by still other people . . . It seemed like, at some point, the world would just get filled up with all kinds of people working at jobs they'd rather not be doing. And all sorts of things. I drove home.

I finally got my telephone. I went in to the telephone co-op office the next day and paid the security deposit, hook-up fee, telephone damage deposit, a year's co-op membership dues, and applicable taxes. I bought a firing pin and box of ammunition for my rifle and put a couple dollars of gas in the truck. That left me with about eight bucks. Oh well. I was still ahead.

The next day the phone company called the Llano Alto post office and left a message saying they'd be there on Friday, maybe Monday, to run a line to the house and hook up my phone. They came the following Wednesday.

It really didn't matter. I had a telephone and I drove up and down the valley, stopping at all the stores, ranchers' homes, and businesses.

I gave my phone number to all of them and asked them to call if they had any work. I went home and waited for a call.

In the meantime, I busied myself around my grandmother's farm fixing fences, straightening and re-hanging the outhouse door, patching the roof on the sheep barn, splitting firewood, changing the oil in the truck, and painting the trim around the windows and doors of the house. Bennie Maestas came by and hired me to dig a new hole for his outhouse. I was reluctant to get too far from the telephone and left a pad of paper and a pencil on the stand next to it, so my grandmother could write down any messages for me. It took most of two days to dig Bennie's outhouse hole. He paid me ten bucks and lunch.

I went back to working around my grandmother's place, and waited.

It wasn't like the phone never rang. Margarito called a few times to see if I had a job yet and my tía Carolina called every morning and every afternoon to talk to my grandmother. It seemed like after a few days my phone number had gotten pretty well spread around. My grandmother got calls from friends and relatives she hadn't seen in years, from all kinds of places like Albuquerque, Dos Cabezas, Santa Fe, Denver, Long Beach, and both Las Vegases.

I was a little put out about the whole thing. After all, Grandma hadn't even wanted a phone and there I was still waiting for a call offering me a job, which was why I had shoveled garbage for five days and ate lunch alone on the pickup tailgate so I could get the phone in the first place.

I waited.

A whole month passed without a call for me, unless you count Margarito's. It got so that every time I walked past the phone I'd pick up the receiver to check for a dial tone, just to be sure the thing was working.

I was up on the house roof one day trying to straighten out the stovepipe and caulk around where the pipe and the roof tin came together. The pipe was pretty well rusted through so I decided to go to town for some new pipe. I figured I might as well get some groceries and a La Plaza newspaper while I was there.

I drove down to Lebanon's, gathered up a couple sections of eight-inch stovepipe, a small can of roofing tar, a basket of groceries my grandmother had ordered over the phone and made my way to the checkout counter.

"I've been trying to call you," Lebanon said. "I had a job for you but your line was always busy. I went ahead and hired Juan Lopez." I didn't say anything.

Lebanon was sold out of newspapers so I drove over to Lynch's store.

"Something must be wrong with your phone," Roberto Lynch said. "I had a plumbing job for you and tried to call but it seems like your line's always busy. I called Bennie Garcia instead."

It was all pretty discouraging.

On my way home I stopped by the post office and picked up the mail. Della told me that I had a postage due envelope from the telephone company. I gave her twelve cents and she handed me a thick letter which I placed on top of the stack of my grandmother's usual junk mail. The telephone company envelope had one of those little plastic windows with my name and address behind it and "OPEN IMEDITELY" written in big red magic-marker letters on the front.

I sat in the truck, ran my pocket knife blade under the crease of the envelope and pulled out the stack of papers.

It was a "TERMINATION NOTICE" and a bill for $352.23. Payable within fifteen days from the date of the notice. I had ten dollars and ten days left. I couldn't figure it out.

I looked at the list of calls and charges on page two, and page three, and page four of the bill. There were all kinds of collect calls from all over New Mexico and five different states, and long-distance calls to at least three different countries.

I didn't go home right away. I slowly drove up the valley, past the last house, into the canyon, got off the truck and bellowed. I kicked a rock.

I think I broke my toe but it really didn't matter, I still couldn't afford to see a doctor or go to the hospital. I limped back to the truck, got on, and drove home.

My grandmother couldn't understand it when I showed her the bill. It seemed like somebody had told her you didn't have to pay for collect phone calls. Worse, she had somehow gotten the idea that she was going to "collect" something (she had no idea what) from all the phone calls she had been getting. I tried to explain "collect calls" to her and how the person receiving the call had to pay and . . . I finally gave up.

"What about these calls to France and Germany?" I asked her. "And Israel. Who do you know in Israel?"

"I don't know who those people are," she replied, all thoughtful. "Most of them didn't even speak Spanish or English. But that girl in Israel, she spoke good English and was very nice. She said I could call her again." She smiled at the thought of it. I shuddered.

"How did you . . ." I stopped right there. Her junk mail was always full of ads, addresses, and telephone numbers.

It really wasn't that important. There was no way I was going to earn enough money in ten days to pay that bill. My telephone would get terminated and I wouldn't get a job. And my toe throbbed. I unplugged the phone and put a bag of ice on my foot before going to bed that night.

The next morning, I tossed the phone onto the truck seat and headed to the co-op in La Plaza. I stopped at Lebanon's, on the way through town, to get a candy bar. I figured it would probably be the last one I could afford for a while.

"What happened to your foot?" Lebanon asked as I limped through the door.

I told him.

He laughed and told me to follow him. He led me to his office in a back corner of the store.

"I've got to get to La Plaza," I said. "Before they send somebody out here to pick up the phone and charge me another twenty bucks."

He insisted that I sit. I did.

Lebanon opened his big black walk-in safe, rummaged in it for a minute, and turned toward me with a stack of money in his hand. He counted out four hundred-dollar bills and dropped them on his desk in front of me.

"I can't take that. There's no way I can pay you back," I moaned.

"Are you sure? I thought you wanted to work." He had me there.

And that's how I paid off the telephone bill and why I spent the next couple months working for Lebanon. I tried to give Lebanon the $47.77 that was left over after I paid off the phone bill. He refused it and called us even. I guess my phone did help me get a job after all.

Even better, I got to keep the phone and used part of the $47.77 to treat my grandmother to dinner at Roberto's.

She had the enchiladas, with red.

MARGARITO AND SOLO VINO

My friend, Margarito Montoya, stands barely five-foot-six in his boots. His simple clothes and quiet manner are deceiving. He can work all day digging a ditch or toss sixty-five-pound bales of hay to the height of a pickup cab in the morning, shear sheep all afternoon, and play lively waltzes all evening on his guitar. He's at least thirty years older than me and I've tried my best to keep up with him, except for the lively waltz part. Most of my life I've been musically challenged. But that's another story.

When Margarito speaks, his hands flitter dart wave and punctuate the air around him with his mood. At times they're as light and sudden as pajaritos taking flight. At other times they are as dark and serious as ravens against a New Mexico winter sky. When he plays a guitar . . . his hands reveal his soul.

He keeps a flock of sheep that number between eight and twenty, depending on how many ewes have lambed and whether or not they've had twins, and one ram. His sheep are direct descendants of his ancestors' flocks that once numbered in the hundreds. He can relate at length the lineage of each.

When lambing season arrives, he closes the flock up day and night in a coyote-proof log and wire corral. At other times of the year, they graze sixteen acres of irrigated pasture that slopes gradually up, from behind his house, to the pine-covered hills surrounding the Llano Alto valley.

His home is a comfortable generations-old three-room L-shaped adobe with a steeply pitched tin roof. A covered portal runs the length of the long side of the L. Each room has a door to the outside, and a few yards downhill the Río Pequeño flows playfully by. He shares his home with a large gray battle-scarred yellow-eyed shaggy-bearded dog he named Solo Vino.

Solo Vino or, as we call him, Solo, arrived one year at Margarito's house the day after Thanksgiving. The way Margarito tells it, he had been asleep and was awakened sometime during the night by the sound of a violin outside his bedroom window. He went to the door and flung it open, eager to greet the violinist. Nothing. Nobody.

He called out. Still nothing.

He went back to bed and had just drifted off to sleep when the sound of the violin awakened him again. This time it was coming from the front of the house. He rose and ran to the kitchen door. He hesitated a moment before opening it, and listened. The violinist was playing an old waltz. One of his favorites. One he hadn't heard in many years.

He eased the door open and stuck his head out. Again, nothing.

Afraid he might be losing his mind he returned to bed and pulled a pillow over his head.

No sooner had he gotten comfortable than, once again, the violinist began playing a tune Margarito remembered from his youth. One his grandfather had composed. This time he refused to leave the bed. He shouted, "Whoever you are, feel free to come in from the cold. The doors are not locked." And, he thought to himself, how do you know my grandfather's music?

The next morning, he rose, wrapped up in a heavy blanket against the chill, stepped out the back door and started as usual to the outhouse. The clear morning air smelled of cold and burning piñon. Thin blue ribbons of smoke from the night's fires hung in the still air just above rooftops. The young sun barely touched the tops of the hills, painting them a delicate glittering golden pink. Just outside the door, in the thick frost that coated the ground and everything else, he saw a trail of large indistinct footprints. Margarito couldn't tell if the prints had been made by a person or an animal wandering around the house during the night. He shuffled quickly to the outhouse and before stepping inside looked cautiously around. Despite the cold he left the door open a few inches so that he could see out. Just in case he'd missed something. Or someone.

He listened for any unusual sound. Nothing. He kept watch through the partly open door for any unusual activity. Still nothing. He finished, stepped out, turned toward the house, and stopped. The bedroom door was open. He was sure he had closed it.

Margarito hurried to the house, unlaced boots flopping loosely around his ankles. He paused only for a moment to choose a piece of piñon from the woodpile that would do as a club. Weapon in hand, he strode into the bedroom. No one.

He let the blanket slide from his shoulders onto a chair, closed the door, and started toward the kitchen with the makeshift club in his hand.

Someone was snoring. Loud. Margarito tightened his grip on the club and peered around the corner. Nobody.

He slowly slipped into the kitchen, and froze in surprise. Lying on the floor in front of Bertha, his black and chrome Home Comfort wood cookstove, was a big shaggy gray dog. Melting ice dripped from the dog's coat, making little puddles of water on the floor around him. The dog snorted in his sleep, stretched, and resumed snoring. He didn't even open his eyes. Margarito just stood there, trying to understand how this could have happened.

Finally, he roused himself and cautiously made his way over to the woodbox. A single bushy-browed yellow eye followed him, then closed, obviously unconcerned. Margarito just sat there on a corner of the woodbox trying to think what to do. The piñon club seemed suddenly heavy and out of place. He lightly dropped it into the box and decided that he'd let the poor creature warm up, feed him, and send him on his way.

By the time I arrived in Llano Alto, Margarito and Solo had been sharing breakfasts of bacon, huevos, papas fritas, and tortillas every morning for more or less five years.

Margarito is a well-known musician and ethnomusicologist. He's pretty famous in certain circles as a guitarist and preserver of traditional New Mexico music: valses, Inditas, cunas, taleans, cuadrillas, and the like. Every once in a while, he travels to play and speak at venues in different cities and towns. When he's out of town, I feed and water his sheep, feed Solo, and look after his home.

It's no big deal and pretty much the same routine I follow every day at my grandmother's. Actually, I'm glad for something to do since I'd given up hope of finding a full- time job and I might as well spend time helping out my friend.

Every night I would close the sheep in the barn to keep them safe from predators like coyotes, bears, and mischief-seeking dogs. In the morning I fed them from a stack of sweet-smelling grass and alfalfa hay spread out in a trough made from the hollowed-out half of a cottonwood log. A two-pound coffee can full of grain gets sprinkled out on top of the hay. Usually, the sheep get water from the acequia or the Río Pequeño but when Margarito is out of town, I keep them penned up in the corral and haul water from the río to a trough made from an old water heater tank cut lengthwise in half. It's not exactly rocket science.

Late one night, Margarito called and asked if I would feed his sheep and take care of Solo for a few days. I was a little groggy. It was after midnight and I'd been asleep for at least three hours. It seemed that he had to go out of town to lecture about traditional Spanish music at a community college in Tucson or Phoenix, someplace like that. He'd meant to tell me earlier but it had somehow slipped his mind. His cousin Lario was going to drive him to the airport in Albuquerque that afternoon. I told him I'd be glad to help and I'd be over in the morning to see him off. Just before he hung up, he added a closing comment, "Oh, and I have a revelation for you."

I wished he hadn't said that. And why had he called so late? His "revelation" comment and the lateness of the hour concerned me. I couldn't get back to sleep and lay in bed wide awake, for at least an hour, trying to figure out what his "revelation" could be about.

The next morning, I jumped out of bed before my grandmother was awake, fed her sheep and dogs, started a fire in the kitchen stove, skipped my usual breakfast, and headed over to Margarito's. I breakfasted on a cold tortilla washed down with a very black, very nasty cup of lukewarm instant coffee as I drove. The sun was barely peeking over Sierra Rota at the east end of the valley. It was already a beautiful day. Perfect for seeking my friend's "revelation."

Second to music, Margarito is passionate about color. Not in his clothing or anything like that. He usually wears simple Western-cut dime-store shirts and second-hand jeans. It's his house. Each wall, each piece of furniture, each window, each door, each coffee cup, even each plate is an element in a barely-controlled explosion of apparently random colors. And they change at a whim.

I strode along the portal toward its far end and the open kitchen door. Aromatic blue piñon smoke from Bertha's stovepipe curled lazily around the eaves of the portal. The door wore a fresh coat of lavender paint that would make a lilac blush. I was sure it had been bright blue just a couple weeks ago. I stepped through the doorway into the kitchen.

The walls glowed with an ecstatic yellow frenzy in the morning light that streamed through the east window. Apparently, he had taken advantage of the same paint sale at Lebanon's store as my grandmother. Solo was lying in his usual spot on the floor in front of Bertha. A blue enamel coffee pot hissed happily on the stove. A rhythmic swishing sound hinted that somewhere, somebody was sweeping. I called out, "Hello, 's me." No answer. I tried again, "Uh, buenos días?"

Margarito pirouetted from behind Bertha, humming a vals, hands wrapped lightly around a red-handled broom that he called "Lisa." Actually, Margarito calls all his brooms Lisa. He's waltzed through household chores with several over the years and good-naturedly complains that none of the narrow-waisted vixens have had the stamina to keep step with him for more than a few months. They just wear out.

Lisa made an elegant pass between Solo and Bertha, picking up a handful of dried mud on the way. Solo didn't move. With one fluid motion Margarito stood Lisa against the wall and gestured for me to take a seat at the table. He mumbled a barely audible "buenos días."

I just stood there, waiting for the promised revelation. He gestured again for me to take a seat and poured coffee into a lime green cup that he set on the table beside a blue plate piled four high with bizcochitos. I sat in the red chair. It was closest to the cinnamon and anise flavored cookies that were my favorites.

He hastily set an orange cup of coffee on the table, nearly spilling the contents, and dropped into the chair across from me. He just sat there for a moment looking at his unusually still hands. I was worried. Margarito never almost-spilled anything, and his hands were rarely still. I took a bizcochito, dunked it in my coffee, and waited.

When my friend finally spoke, he didn't look up from his hands. "Do you know the story of my grandfather Salodonio?"

I lifted the bizcochito. It was dangerously close to falling apart. I carefully slipped it into my mouth. "No." It was all I could manage around a mouthful of soggy bizcochito.

He looked at me and smiled indulgently. "Good, huh?" I nodded. "Roberta Rodriguez made them. She brought them by yesterday."

I lifted another from the plate and considered whether to eat it dunked or dry.

"You know how I've felt for a while that something is different about Solo?" he asked, all serious.

I nodded. Margarito had told me one night, while we were driving home from La Plaza, that something about Solo had changed. My friend had come to believe that the spirit of some one or some thing had taken up residence in the dog. I wasn't exactly ready to accept that, but I'll admit Solo was different. I just more or less figured that regular meals and lying around all day in the sun or in front of Bertha were making him lazy. He was getting fat, too.

Then I remembered the first time I met Solo. He'd been lying in front of Bertha. He had raised his head and just looked at me with those yellow eyes. I got the creepy feeling that he was trying to tell me something. Apparently, I was too dense to get it because he gave up after a minute or two and settled back down to the floor with a groan, closed his eyes, and resumed snoring.

Margarito continued slowly. "Yesterday, when I was practicing, right before they called from Tucson to remind me about the lecture, a strange thing happened." He was looking at his hands again.

He told me that he'd been playing an Indita on his guitar when all of a sudden, Solo, who was lying in his other usual spot, the rug in the bedroom where Margarito practices, suddenly sat up and started singing. Margarito had nearly dropped his guitar from the surprise of it. At first, he thought it was a coincidence, just something that dogs do sometimes, but Solo went on singing all by himself until he finished the song. Margarito just sat there, arm draped over his guitar, staring at the dog in disbelief. He swore that his grandfather Salodonio looked back at him from behind the Solo's bushy-browed eyes.

Margarito had eventually collected himself and continued with his practice. Solo sang along with him on each song, for over an hour. He eventually tired, lay down, and went back to sleep.

During the night, Margarito had been awakened three times. Each time he thought he heard someone playing a violin outside the house. Just like the night before Solo had arrived. When he opened the door, no one was there, and the music stopped. Each time he found Solo snoring in his sleep, in front of Bertha.

Margarito shook his head slowly. "I think that my grandfather Salodonio is in Solo, or Solo is Salodonio or . . . whatever. I don't know." His eyes didn't leave his hands.

He lifted the orange cup and took a sip of coffee. I put on my best poker face to hide my doubt. If he had looked up at me it wouldn't have helped much though. I never have won a game of poker.

"My grandfather, Salodonio Valdez," he said slowly, "was a famous violinista." At least he was looking at me now. "He played for all the bailes and funciones around these parts for many years.

"When Salodonio was ten years old he started out playing a drum with his uncles. He wasn't satisfied just beating on a tambor so he taught himself to play the violin. By the time he was twelve he'd gotten good enough to play a vals or two at a wedding dance. People were amazed by his ability. After that, he was in demand for all the dances and get-togethers."

I glanced at Solo. Margarito took another sip of coffee. Solo groaned in his sleep and stretched out without opening his eyes.

"Salodonio married Lupita Ortiz and they had six children, five that lived." He raised a finger on his left hand. "There was my uncle Juan. He was killed in a car wreck in Albuquerque not long after World War II. My tío Severo"—he raised a second finger—"went to California, Long Beach I think. Nobody's heard from him in years. He might be dead too. Then there's my tía Guadalupe, she lives in Santa Fe, and my mother, and my tía Maria. She lives in Las Vegas with her third husband." He raised a finger for each one as he counted them off.

"By the time Salodonio was about twenty-three, maybe twenty-five, something like that, he had saved up enough money to order a fine European violin. In those days everything that wasn't grown or made in the mountains came by narrow-gauge train to the station in the Río Grande gorge." Margarito waved his hand in the general direction of the river.

"The things that came on the train were brought from the station to Río Pueblo by wagon, over the mountains. My grandmother told me how Salodonio could barely contain his anticipation and excitement over the new violin. Every week he rode with the freighters down to the train station. It was a two or three-day round trip, depending on the weather, and they slept at night beneath the wagons. The freighters never charged Salodonio because he played his violin for them along the way. I have even heard it said that the mules danced all night to the music of his violin and were so tired the next day that they could barely pull the wagon up the hill to Río Pueblo." Margarito laughed.

I was beginning to feel better about my friend's mood and popped another half of a bizcochito into my mouth. I washed it down with the rest of my coffee. Margarito slid out of his chair, stepped around Solo, refilled our coffee cups, and put the pot back on the cooler side of the stove. He sat down and resumed his grandfather's story.

"Finally, the new violin arrived. From everything I've heard it was beautiful and sounded even better than it looked. Nothing like it had ever been seen or heard before in the mountains. The new violin became my grandfather's constant companion.

"Good violinists were always in demand and Salodonio was exceptional. He played the new violin at all the dances and funciones and his reputation grew and spread. Wherever he went, whatever he did, the new violin was with him. After a while people began to call the violin 'la esposa de Salodonio' or just 'la Esposa.'" He realized that he had lost me.

"Oh, right. Esposa would be spouse or wife in English."

I thanked him and he continued. "My grandfather knew all the traditional music and a lot of the new tunes that came to New Mexico with the Americans. He and la Esposa played the Matachines at the pueblos for Christmas, they played for weddings and fiestas, everything. It seems that everybody wanted to hear and dance to the music of Salodonio and la Esposa."

Margarito's eyes had regained their sparkle, fired by the passion for music that he shared with his grandfather. As my friend wove the tale of Salodonio and la Esposa I envisioned gaily dressed people swaying to the voice of la Esposa, dancing to cunas, taleans, la varsoviana, and innumerable valses named in honor of people and musicians from various communities. Cortés, la Malinche, and el Monarca were brought to life in the Matachines through the magic of Salodonio and la Esposa. Newlyweds had been inspired by the devotion between them and religious faith was most certainly fortified by the depths of Salodonio's and la Esposa's passion.

My friend paused for a moment before he continued.

"But I guess even Salodonio couldn't make enough money as a violinista to feed his and Lupita's growing family." Margarito mused. "Maybe he just wasn't good with money. I don't know.

"Anyway, Salodonio, not being a farmer or a stockman, had to find a job so he went to work for a company that was cutting trees in the mountains for railroad ties. In those days, every canyon in the mountains had a sawmill. You can still see pieces of them left over in some places. The men would cut the trees and drag them with teams of horses to the mill where they would cut them into railroad ties. Then they stacked the ties until spring when they floated them, with the runoff from the snowpack, down the canyons to the Río del Indio. Eventually the ties would get to the Río Grande, where they were loaded onto the train, and shipped to Albuquerque. A few years later, they built a railroad up to the valley, and hauled the logs down to larger sawmills.

"Salodonio kept la Esposa close at hand, even in the logging camps. He played every chance he got and nobody complained. One time, they asked him to play for the wedding dance of the mayor's son in La Plaza, so he was practicing a lot. Not that he ever needed a reason. It seemed like my grandfather would rather play music than eat. He even took la Esposa into the mountains with him. That's when it happened." He stopped right there.

I waited.

"What?" I finally blurted out. "What happened?"

He took a long slow drink of coffee before he went on. "The way I heard it was, one day, the men were cutting down a huge pine. Maybe they were in a hurry because it was getting late. Maybe they weren't being as careful as they should have or maybe a wandering gust of wind came along. I don't know. The tree started to lean toward the wagon where the men kept all their tools. And more importantly, where my grandfather kept la Esposa.

"Lorenzo Romero's grandfather ran to the wagon, jumped up on the seat and urged the mules to pull the wagon out of the way. I guess for a few seconds everything looked like it was going to be all right. But the tree twisted, you know how it happens sometimes, and it started to fall again toward the wagon. Lorenzo's grandfather jumped off and ran for his life. When Salodonio realized what was happening he ran as fast as he could toward the wagon and la Esposa. He and the tree got there at the same time. He and the wagon disappeared under the huge trunk and branches.

"Everybody just stood there, like they were frozen. Suddenly, they realized what had happened and all ran over to the wreck. The mules were screaming and kicking and my grandfather was lying there with one of his legs pinned under a branch. The wagon and everything in it, turned to scrap. Some men cut the mules free while others freed Salodonio."

I had a bad feeling. "And la Esposa?" I whispered.

Margarito shook his head. "Her leather-covered case and fine wood were no match for the huge tree. She was broken into a hundred pieces. My grandfather dragged himself over to what was left of her and gathered the pieces up in his jacket. Refusing help for his bleeding and broken leg, he hobbled, alone, back to the logging camp. When I was young, I heard a rumor that he buried the remains of la Esposa in a corner of the church graveyard. But I don't know if it's true or not."

I sat back in my chair and wiped at my eyes.

"My grandfather's leg healed crooked and after that he always walked with a limp. Everybody could tell when a storm was coming and how severe it would be by how badly Salodonio limped. He found another violin from somewhere, maybe it was his old one, and continued to do his duty for the people. But . . . it was never the same without la Esposa. It seemed like his spirit just withered away after that. My grandmother finally got fed up with his moroseness and moved to her sister's in Santa Fe. She took all the children, except my mother who was already married, with her.

"For years, people all around told the story of Salodonio and la Esposa. Mothers used the story to admonish children not to put love of fame and material things before their family. I've always wondered why nobody seemed to remember how much they had enjoyed the music of Salodonio and la Esposa, or how devoted he was to her and their music. It seems like my whole life, I've lived with the ghosts of my grandfather and la Esposa."

I lifted another bizcochito from the plate and dunked it in my coffee. If I had thought that was the end of it, I was wrong.

"My grandfather was pretty old when I knew him. He didn't play the violin in public anymore. One time, when I was about ten years old, we went to see him. He took out his violin and played a song for me. I never heard that song again . . . until the night before Solo came to live with me. It must have been one of my grandfather's own compositions. That day at my grandfather's, I decided that I wanted to play the violin too. Just like him. But my mother wouldn't hear of it."

His voice was barely audible. I had to lean close to hear him. "I guess that's why I play the guitar."

He paused for minute, maybe two. Solo drew a long, deep breath.

"Eventually, Salodonio just wandered off. Nobody knows when or where he went. It was just . . . one day he was there and the next day he was gone. Nobody ever saw him again, but every once in a while, we would hear a story from a hunter or a sheepherder how, at certain times in the night, they had heard a violin singing in the canyons. Echoing, deep in the mountains. They were always sure it was Salodonio and la Esposa."

The clock on the wall beside Bertha ticked. Loud in the silence. The dying fire in the stove muttered. Even Solo had stopped snoring. Damn, I wanted to cry. It was that sad.

Half of the coffee-soaked bizochito fell from my hand and plopped into the cup, splashing coffee on the table. It broke the mood. We looked at each other and smiled.

A bizcochito appeared suddenly in Margarito's hand. "Mira," he said, and tossed it onto the linoleum floor between him and Solo. It landed so lightly that it didn't even crack. Solo yawned, opened his eyes, stood and took a few steps toward it. He was limping, barely putting any weight on his right hind leg.

"What the . . ." I said incredulously and turned toward Margarito. He just nodded. A smile rippled across his face.

The next morning, I drove over to Margarito's house to do the chores. Solo was still limping so I lifted his right hind leg to look for a grass burr or a cut. He growled and bared his teeth. I left him alone and he limped off to lay down in the morning sun. That night it rained.

A couple nights later Margarito called to tell me he was home. It was late and I'd been asleep, again. Just before he hung up, he said, "I have another revelation for you."

I didn't care how late it was. I dressed right then and drove over to his house.

The light was on in the kitchen. The door stood open. I jumped up on the porch and hurried toward the open door and the sound of a violin playing a soft, slow waltz.

BLACKSMITHS

MARGARITO AND I DECIDED to drive back from Santa Fe, where he had bought some strings for his guitar and violin, on the mountain road. The two-lane shoulderless highway winds through high-altitude forests: tall pines and firs on the north slopes, piñons, junipers, and cactus on the south-facing slopes. Each secluded valley sheltered a cluster of steep-roofed adobe homes and leaning log barns that would suddenly appear as we rounded a curve or dropped off a hill.

It was mid-June. The truck windows were down and the cool mountain air flowed through the cab. Neither of us had much to say. We were just enjoying the afternoon. To the east, the mountains glittered, above timberline, with the remnants of last winter's snowpack. Thin foamy rivulets of snowmelt wandered idly through bar ditches and arroyos. Winter's lethargic brown was grudgingly giving way to summer's vibrant green. The only vehicle we'd passed in the last five miles was a muddy sixty-something Chevy pickup with a few bales of moldy hay, left over from winter, in the bed. The moustached driver in a battered black hat waved as we passed. We waved back.

Around a tight curve and down a hill, just north of the La Plaza County line, we dropped into a small town of about a dozen residences. The cluster of adobe homes, remains of the original fortified plaza, was overshadowed by the church that stood on a rise across the narrow valley. The church was one of the remaining few in the state that had not been plastered over with stucco. It stood tall, silent, earth-colored. The same earth from which it had been built nearly three hundred years ago. Twin bell towers stretched upward to soft fluffy clouds in a deep blue sky.

"Pull over there. In front of the church." Margarito said suddenly. He waved his hand in a general direction that included the north third of the state.

I jerked the wheel to the right and we skidded to a stop in the dust and gravel of the plaza, more or less facing the church. We barely missed two mixed-breed dogs that slunk off, wide eyed, tails between their legs.

A low adobe wall surrounded the church and enclosed an ancient graveyard. Wood and iron grave markers leaned at various angles. I shut off the engine. Silence closed in around us.

"You see that ironwork? On top of the crosses, the gate, the door hinges?" Margarito asked animatedly. His hands sketched vague directions in the air.

I scrunched down and looked out through the remains of splattered bugs and cracks in the windshield.

"Uh huh," I replied. I leaned out the open side window to get a less obstructed view.

"My great grandfather made all that. He was a blacksmith. I have all his tools there at the house."

"Really? Where?" I didn't remember seeing anything that faintly resembled a forge or blacksmith shop at his home.

"That little shed, over by the sheep pen. It's all in there." He explained. "My bisabuelo was a pretty famous blacksmith. He made all the iron work for all the churches in the mountains. The old church in Río Pueblo too, but it was all lost when the church burned. He even made most of his own tools, shoed horses, fixed wagons and . . . everything." Margarito was obviously proud of his heritage.

"No kidding?" I really was fascinated by the thought of hand-forging iron into usable tools and decorations. "You know how to do it?"

"Well, not like my bisabuelo but I learned a few tricks when I was young. I made the hinges for the gate in the sheep corral but I haven't made anything for a while. Why?"

"Well, I was thinking that I might learn to make something simple, like a knife, or some hinges for a shed or something like that." I struggled to keep the pleading tone out of my voice. "If someone would teach me."

"We can do that. Easy. How about tomorrow?" he offered.

I didn't hesitate. "What time?"

"Whenever. I'll be home all day. Bring some gloves, glasses, and a thick shirt."

I started the truck and turned back onto the highway toward home.

It was about seven fifteen the next morning when I drove up to Margarito's house. He was tramping around outside in knee-high black rubber irrigation boots, finishing the morning chores. The sheep were out in the pasture along the Río Pequeño. Solo Vino, a little muddier than usual, was lying in the sun at the edge of the porch.

I looked at the shed with a new respect. It stood between the corrals and the river, almost hidden by capulín and wild plum bushes that had grown up around it. I guess I'd just never paid attention to it before. It was small, about eight by ten and made of very old wood.

If it had ever been painted, the pigment had long since vanished. The boards made a weathered symphony of browns and grays. The door, which was almost as wide as the front of the shed, was pretty elaborate and made of overlaid boards with cutout traditional patterns in them. A huge rust-patinaed padlock hung in a hasp on the door and the roof sloped from the front to the back. I didn't see any windows. A rusty stovepipe protruded from the roof, leaning precariously over the front corner closest to the river.

Margarito strode up to the shed door and drew a large brass ring from his jacket pocket. The solitary key on the ring slid neatly into the lock. He looked at me. "Ready?"

I nodded. The lock clicked open smoothly when he turned the key. He smiled with satisfaction.

"My bisabuelo made this lock and key. This whole shop was his. It used to be over at Ojo Colorado but my father moved it here after his father died. Nobody else in the family wanted any of this stuff."

He waved his hand expansively as he swung open the huge door. The whole structure groaned with the effort to keep from collapsing. Morning sun flooded into the shed. Inside, wooden shelves sagged under the weight of ancient wooden boxes, cans, and tools. A beat-up metal bucket on the floor held even more tools and a pile of coal beckoned invitingly in the morning sun from the back of the shed. A handful of scraggly sun-starved weeds poked up from cracks in the hard-packed dirt floor. Everything was coated with at least a half inch of dust.

Margarito brushed cobwebs out of the doorway. In a front corner were the forge and an anvil that looked like it weighed a hundred and twenty pounds. The anvil was mounted with railroad spikes on a huge section of pine log. Behind the anvil and forge, against the wall, were two barrels that held some dark, dust-coated, slimy, unidentifiable liquids.

"What's in those?" I pointed with my lips toward the barrels.

"Secret family recipes." He answered with exaggerated mystery "For quenching and tempering the iron."

The forge wasn't very big. It was one of those commercial types that I had seen before in barns. Usually, they were rusted through from long disuse, buried beneath mounds of baling twine, empty feed sacks, moth-eaten old sheepskins and rusty discarded truck fenders. The forge stood on spindly legs and there was a hand-operated blower that you cranked to create a draft, instead of a bellows. Ashes from the last time it had been used, probably when Margarito made the hinges, still lay in its shallow metal pan. Except for a few dozen cobwebs, a little rust, and a layer of dust, this one looked like it was in pretty good condition.

Margarito produced a rag from somewhere and began wiping cobwebs and dust from the forge. The roof of the shop was low enough that I had to bend over slightly at the waist to stand at the highest point. I didn't care. I was eager to learn the secrets of blacksmithing and had barely been able to sleep the night before.

When I had finally fallen asleep, visions of my grandchildren, using a knife that I had forged, carving the Christmas ham, came and went. They had waved the knife proudly toward a stoop-shouldered, white-haired old man, me, sitting at the dining table. "This is the knife that Granpo made." They shouted it loud enough for my failing hearing...

"Get a couple handfuls of coal from the back," Margarito instructed.

I pulled my wood cutting, fence fixing, post hole digging gloves on and scuttled to the back of the shed. I lifted the coal in a small shovel that I found lying on top of the pile. I stood up, bumped my head on a viga and dropped half the coal. Margarito chuckled and went to the house. I scooped up the errant pieces and tipped about half the shovelful into the forge. Margarito returned a carrying a worn coffee can. He dug in the can with a spoon.

"Old Indin fire starter trick," he quipped as he tossed a spoonful of kerosene-soaked sawdust onto the coal. He reached for a box of matches on a shelf behind him, removed one from the box and struck it. The match was old and sputtered fitfully as it struggled to life. He carefully dropped it onto the mix of kerosene-soaked sawdust and coal. The mixture burned slowly with a bright blue flame.

"Now what?"

"We wait."

While the fire was burning itself into a red heat, he rummaged through a pile of scrap iron that I had failed to notice in my excitement. He stood up suddenly, a horn-handled pocket knife in his hand. He held it up to the light and grinned like a treasure hunter who'd found the treasure of the Sierra Madre.

"So, that's what happened to this knife." He held it so I could see. "I looked all over for this. I lost it a couple years ago and had to buy another one at Lynch's store." He slid the knife into his pants pocket and returned to rummaging in the pile.

He looked over his shoulder at the forge and told me to crank the handle a bit. "Slowly, just enough to get it burning real good. And toss a little more fire starter on it."

I did and the coal crackled into flame, yellow-white in the center, fading to red, then blue-black at the outer edges.

Margarito stood with a piece of rusted iron in his hand. It was about eight inches long and a quarter inch thick. "Got it." He held out the piece of iron to me. "Here's your knife."

I thought he was a little premature but I gave the handle another crank or two. The coal crackled and spat sparks at me. Margarito handed me the piece of iron and started lifting tools from a bucket. He set a pair of long-handled tongs beside the anvil.

"You'll need those. And this." He pulled a short-handled sledgehammer from the bucket and dropped it on the anvil. The steel rang.

I hefted the bar of iron in my hand, trying to envision the knife that lay in there, somewhere. The thought crossed my mind that my grandchildren might need to buy a carving knife from the store.

Margarito stood for a minute looking into the bucket of tools. "There should be a smaller hammer here somewhere." He bent over again and rummaged deeper in the bucket.

With the morning sun and the heat from the forge, the shop was starting to get pretty warm. The smoke from the fire built up under the roof and rolled placidly out, around the top edge of the doorway, into the morning air. The stovepipe seemed pretty much useless.

Margarito picked up a few pieces of coal and laid them in strategic locations around the fire. I turned the crank slowly to get them burning good. Sparks flew and landed on the floor where they winked knowingly at me before they went dark.

He reached up to a shelf and pulled down a wooden box with a mixture of what looked like dried horse manure, dirt, and grass.

"What's that?"

"I don't know for sure. I think you sprinkle it on the hot iron and fold it over with the hammer. To add carbon to the iron." He set the box aside. "Or something like that," he mumbled.

"Looks like a rat's nest to me."

I continued slowly cranking the handle for a few more minutes while he poked around in the boxes and wiped dust off the shelves.

"That looks about right," he pronounced after a few minutes. He lifted the piece of iron from my hand with the long-handled tongs and pushed it deep into the heart of the fire.

"Turn the handle," he instructed.

I did. The edges of the iron bar were already turning red.

"When the whole thing gets red, take it out with the tongs, put it on the anvil, and hammer it into the shape you want."

"Just like that?" I asked.

"Yeah. It's not rocket science. And watch out for sparks. Where are your glasses?"

I had forgotten them in my excitement. I pulled from my jacket pocket a pair of sunglasses that I had borrowed last night from my grandmother's purse when she was asleep.

"That's all you have?"

"Well, yeah that's all I have. I don't wear glasses." I slipped them on. The inside of the shed went dark.

"Well, I guess they're better than nothing," he conceded. "But don't blame me if you put an eye out."

Through the glasses I could see only the half of him that was in direct sunlight. The rest of him and the interior of the shed were dark, green-black shadows. I turned back to the forge. The heart of the thing glowed like a yellow-green dragon's eye. I couldn't tell if the iron was red or not. It looked like it might be.

"Is that right?" I asked him, trying to sound like I was asking his advice instead of being half blind.

I felt him lean around me and look into the forge. He turned the crank a couple times and pronounced that it was ready.

I had to lift the glasses to locate the tongs and left them on my forehead so I could find the anvil and hammer. When I located them, I raised the iron from the fire. The coal popped. Sparks flew. I flicked my head and dropped the glasses over my eyes. Margarito stepped back into the dark.

I managed to get about three solid hits on the iron before he told me to put it back in the fire. I repeated the process three or four times. Each time I struck the iron, glowing pieces of metal and sparks flew onto the dirt floor. The anvil rang reassuringly and I was beginning to think that my grandkids might get their knife after all.

Margarito told me to keep working with the bar until I had it hammered thin and even.

"Then you have to fold it over and over until it's ready."

I worked on the bar of iron for about an hour. It was beginning to take on a vague, uneven blade-like shape. I was working up quite a sweat.

"How do you temper it?" I asked.

"Get it real hot and drop it in that barrel over there."

"The secret recipe barrel?"

"Uh huh. Try it. It won't hurt it."

I stuck my vaguely knife-shaped iron bar into the coals and cranked the handle until the iron was glowing a bright yellowish white, even through the sunglasses. Margarito stood reassuringly next to me as I lifted it from the forge. I lifted the sunglasses to find the barrel and dropped the blade into the slime-covered liquid.

Ka-whooom! The barrel exploded in a flash of flame.

I was blinded by the brightness of the explosion. Grandma's sunglasses went flying. Margarito went flying. I went flying and landed half on Margarito.

My face was hot. I could smell burning hair. The sunglasses had vanished. I looked up at the shed. The whole place was a ball of flame. Margarito pushed me off of him and sat up. "Agua, get water!" he shouted hysterically.

I turned toward him and saw that the front of his jacket was burning. He rolled over and smothered the flames. I staggered to my feet, ran to the sheep corral, unhooked the water bucket, and ran to the river.

The river was about thirty feet from the blacksmith shed and by the time I had run back a lot of the fire had died down. It was mostly burning around the remnants of the secret recipe barrel. Margarito had produced a shovel from somewhere and was throwing dirt on the flames as fast as he could. I tossed the water on a flaming wall and ran back to the river for more.

Twenty frantic trips to the river and a hundred shovelfuls of dirt later we had the fire reduced to a few wisps of smoke. My arms felt like they had stretched six inches. Margarito moaned and held his hands to his back. His face was black with soot and dirt. Singed hair curled up from his forehead. His eyebrows were gone. His jacket gave off faint wisps of smoke.

"What did you do that for?" Margarito shouted. "Mira!" He waved his arms in the air like angry flames. "You nearly burned down my grandfather's shop."

"You told me to put it in the barrel," I shouted back. "Secret recipe! What the hell was in there?"

"You . . ." He stopped suddenly, mouth open, dropped to the ground and rolled onto his back, one singed arm over his eyes. I wasn't sure if he was laughing or crying.

He sat up. "You should see yourself." He laughed and pointed at me.

I turned the water bucket over and sat down on it.

"Well, you should see *your* self. What was in that barrel?"

"I just remembered. It was old gasoline from the truck. Remember when I got water in the tank and had to drain it a couple years ago? I didn't know what to do with it so I put it in the shed, in that barrel. I must have forgotten about it. Good thing it wasn't too much, mostly old oil. That's probably when I lost this knife too." He patted the pocket where he had deposited the newfound knife.

We spent twenty more minutes checking for hot spots and thoroughly drowning anything that might even remotely look like a spark. I told Margarito as we worked that I hoped he didn't take it personally but I was going to put my blacksmithing career on hold for a few years. He said that was probably a good idea and suggested that we go get something to eat.

I never did find my grandmother's sunglasses. As Margarito and I bounced along in the truck, turned onto the pavement, and headed toward lunch at Roberto's Café, I made a mental note to stop at Lebanon's store on the way home and get her another pair.

She didn't use them that much. Maybe she wouldn't notice the difference.

MAYBELLE

Margarito's cousin Lario was a pretty laidback guy. There just wasn't much that got to him. He played the cards of life as they were dealt, knew what he needed, what he wanted, and what he could live without. His family always came first.

Lario and his wife, Alice, lived past my grandmother's house, up the road that runs along the side of the llano, then down, across the Río Pequeño. About a quarter mile past the curve, make a right at the Y. Their house was the second one on the right. The one with two cows, a half dozen sheep, and a bay horse in a log corral. Sometimes, the animals might be in the pasture between the house and the river. If Lario's lime-green and yellow metal-flake low rider and sixty-two Chevy pickup were in the yard, he was home. Unless the horse was gone.

Lario and Alice's long low-roofed adobe faced east, toward Sierra Rota and the morning sun. Every room in the house had a view of the mountain. Each year, Lario, Alice, and the kids worked on the house. It fairly glowed with all the attention, its white walls highlighted by bright yellow trim around the windows and doors. In summer, the portal that ran along the length of the east side was nearly obscured by red, yellow, and white varas de San Jose, marigolds, and blue morning glories. The whole place shimmered joyfully from all the comfort, care, and general good feelings.

Lario never worked at any job for more than a month, sometimes two. But he always had work. He had a reputation around the valley as a mechanic, woodcutter, mason, stockman, painter, roofer, plumber, gardener, woodcarver, and furniture maker. He could do just about anything. And everything he did, he did well.

I knew he and Alice had a batch of kids but I never could tell for sure how many. Every summer the manicured yard was full of their kids and a bunch of miniature cousins, nieces, nephews, and neighbors running around with cookies, homemade popsicles, or cheese in their hands. In winter the house was littered with board games, coloring books, colored pencils, homemade toys, and books. Lots of books.

Unlike most everybody else in Llano Alto, Lario and Alice didn't have a dog. They had a puppy once that wandered out into the road. Alice insisted that she just wasn't going to go through all the tears and crying again.

Lario and Alice had one of the biggest and best gardens in Llano Alto. I guess they needed it to feed all those kids. But that in itself couldn't explain it. They always seemed to grow the best corn, the biggest calabacitas, the sweetest havas, and more apples, peaches, and apricots than anyone in the valley. When everyone else's fruit trees froze out, they had fruit. All the nieces, nephews, and neighbor kids helped out with the harvest and Alice always put up whole shelves full of dried, preserved fruits and gallon jars full of chicos, calabacitas, and havas. Every fall Lario would slaughter a hog. Their matanza was an occasion attended by family and neighbors—all of whom took part in the process and shared in the bounty. It was the second most talked-about event in the valley. After the fiestas of course.

One year, Lario decided he was going to get a calf that he planned to raise in his pasture by the river, add a little corn to its diet, and slaughter it in the fall. Lario, Alice, and the kids all piled on the truck one Sunday afternoon and, horse trailer in tow, drove over the mountain to a ranch near Dos Cabezas where he had done some work in exchange for the calf.

Lario figured out pretty quick that he should have left the kids home. He picked a good-sized steer that would feed out with a minimum of cost and effort but somehow, in all the excitement of it, the kids had gotten the idea they were there to pick out a pet. Right away they settled on a small red and white heifer calf that for some reason or other they immediately named Maybelle.

The kids got Maybelle. Lario's plan got put on hold.

He more or less figured the kids would eventually get tired of petting, brushing, riding, and cooing over Maybelle and he'd finally be able to fill his freezer with beef. It didn't work out that way. Once, he mentioned slaughtering Maybelle to Alice. Just once. It seems like she had gotten fond of seeing the now nearly full-grown Maybelle from her kitchen window.

Maybelle had grown up to be gentle, trusting, and easy to get along with. She was halter broke and the kids took turns leading her around the yard while three or four laughing urchins rode on her long broad back.

Lario eventually got to the point where he admitted to himself that Maybelle was a part of the family. Actually, she was the biggest part of the family. She might have started out small but all the attention and extra feed had done their job. Maybelle grew into a fine, fat cow. Well, actually she grew into a fine, fat, four-year old heifer. The one thing missing from Maybelle's life was a calf of her own.

I don't know if Maybelle ever thought about it. A calf of her own, I mean. I'm not even sure what cows think about when they're not eating, drinking, or being chased around by humans trying to brand, tag, vaccinate, or eat them but I know that cows are generally better mothers than some people. Whether Maybelle thought about a calf or not, Margarito did.

Or at least he did the night we brought home a gallon jug of Ted Archuleta's chokecherry wine.

We hadn't really planned on bringing home a jug of wine. We'd spent most of the day installing a door and generally fixing up Ted's half above, half below-ground shed that he used as a root cellar. It turned out that Ted didn't have any money to pay us so we took a paper shopping sack of carne seca and the jug of homemade chokecherry wine in trade.

Margarito and I stopped by for dinner with my grandmother. We gave her half the dried meat and the three of us shared a modest glass of Ted's wine. Shortly after the sun set, it started raining, not too heavy, just nice and steady, so I drove Margarito, the jug of wine and the rest of the carne seca to his house. He invited me in for another glass of wine . . .

It got pretty late. We had been steadily working our way through the sack of carne seca, washed down with glasses of wine, trying to think of where we might be able to pick up some more work. This time for cash.

I think it was somewhere between the second third and the middle of the jug when we got on the subject of Maybelle. We had gone through all the job possibilities we could think of and had somehow wandered onto the topics of social injustices and animal cruelty. Margarito, being the concerned person he normally is, mentioned how it just didn't seem right that "pobrecita Maybelle" had never known a bull and subsequently never had a calf of her own to raise and love.

"Tha'ss right," I heard myself respond. "Po' Maybelle." What I'd meant to say was something along the lines of "it's not our problem." Not that it would have mattered. I think what brought it up was how we had noticed that afternoon, while we were at Lario's returning a saw we had borrowed to do the work at Ted's, that Maybelle was in heat. The three of us were just standing there on the porch drinking the last of a glass of iced tea, watching Maybelle pace back and forth in her corral. Margarito had mentioned to Lario that maybe he should get Maybelle bred. Lario had replied with something like, "It would probably do her good. She's already getting too fat."

"Typical men. You try carrying a child and giving birth!" It was Alice. The three of us typical men jumped and turned. She was standing there in the kitchen doorway, dish towel in her hands, scowling at the three of us. We hadn't even known she was there. Alice went back in the house to whatever it is women do in the afternoon. Margarito and I left.

"You know? We would be doing a favor for Lario, if Maybelle got bred," Margarito suggested.

"Yeah, he's always doing things for us, lending us his tools, showing us how to do things—" I lost my train of thought for a minute. "How we gonna do that?" It seemed like a valid question to me.

"Juan Trujillo."

"Huh?"

"A bull. Juan Trujillo has a bull and he lives just down the road from Lario."

"You heard Alice. She'd never go for it." I'll admit it. I was a little awed by Alice when she was angry.

"Nobody has to know." My friend's eyes sparkled with mischief.

"How?"

The short of it was that he'd been thinking about it all through dinner and the ride home and most of the bag of carne seca and most of half the jug of wine and more or less come up with a plan. The way he figured it, we could sneak over to Lario's, slip a rope halter over Maybelle, and lead her down the road to Juan Trujillo's bull. Then, after the deed was done, we'd just walk Maybelle home, put her back in the corral, and leave.

"Easy, just like taking her on a date." His hands waved and darted in the air with excitement as he laid it all out.

"Too many what ifs," I wanted to say. But I didn't. Besides, Lario and Alice were both really good shots and wouldn't hesitate to shoot a couple of cattle rustlers and ask questions later.

It must have been the wine. Suddenly it seemed to me like it might work and it would be a pretty good thing to do, if we got away with it. Maybelle would get a calf to raise and love, Lario would get a calf to slaughter, and Alice and the kids could still keep Maybelle. I downed the last of my glass of wine. "When you wanna do it?"

"Now. The rain will cover our tracks." He jumped up from his chair and headed for the door. I grabbed my jacket and stumbled after him. We headed out on foot, stopping to pick up a rope as we passed the sheep pens.

Somehow, we managed to slip and slide our way down the road. It was raining pretty heavy and by the time we were halfway to Lario's it had soaked through my jacket and shirt. Caliche mud clung to our boots and made them heavy. The stuff built up two inches thick and made walking pretty tough. It seemed like we just kept moving slower and slower, doing a sort of Boris Karloff mummy shuffle. Neither of us could spare enough breath to talk.

The lights were all out at Lario's when we got there. We were out of breath. It was still raining and I don't think I had a dry spot anywhere. Worse, with all the walking, heavy breathing, mud, and rain I was starting to sober up. Too late . . .

Margarito had hunched down Hollywood-commando style and was making his way through the bushes around the kitchen end of the house, dragging the rope behind him. I followed his lead.

It's a good thing Maybelle was such a pet. We got the rope over her head without any trouble. Margarito threw a couple twists in it so it would work as a halter. I opened the gate and we started off down the road toward Juan Trujillo's bull with Maybelle in tow.

It all went off without a problem. The bull was glad to see Maybelle. Maybelle was glad to see the bull. Margarito and I sat on the ground outside the corral scraping mud from our boots with our pocket knives and waited.

Once it was done, we hitched up Maybelle again and started toward Lario's. We'd only gotten a little way down the road when the bull started making a racket. The lights came on in the Trujillo house. We started running. I slipped and went down face first. Maybelle and Margarito kept on going. A door opened and a flashlight beam wandered around for a minute or two in the rain. I didn't move.

The light winked out and the door closed. A minute later the lights in the house went off. I was up and running.

I got to Lario's just as Margarito was closing the gate. We just stood there looking at each other. Both of us were pretty sober by then and when the realization that we had gotten away with it struck us, we started giggling. We didn't notice it had stopped raining. A light came on in the house and we took off running, cross country.

I lost track of Margarito in the dark and came up at full gallop against a barbed wire fence. I went over like I'd had my legs jerked out from under me, hit the ground, rolled and came up running. A rifle shot cracked in the air. I dropped instinctively and I'd swear I felt the bullet pass by where my head had been just a second before. Maybe it was just the whoosh of my breath as I hit the ground.

I was up and running again in a flash. Somewhere off to my left I could hear thrashing in the thick brush along the banks of the Río Pequeño, then silence. It seemed like a good idea for me to stop too, so I dropped into six of inches of freezing water in the bottom of an irrigation ditch and looked back toward Lario's. I could see him stalking around, rifle in hand, outside the house looking at the tracks we had left in the mud. He bent down and picked something up from the ground then ran off toward Maybelle's corral. Alice shouted from the porch. All I could make out was "Maybelle."

That's when we got our lucky break. The rain started coming down with a vengeance. Lario's house nearly disappeared from sight, it was raining that heavy. I rose from the ditch and started running toward Margarito's.

I don't know how many fences I ran into or crawled through but by the time I got to the house my jeans had a whole bunch of tears in them, my shirt and jacket were torn, my hands were bleeding, and I was spitting mud, grass, and gravel. I stomped onto the porch and headed for the kitchen. Solo Vino was lying in front of the stove. No Margarito. Solo glanced up at me with his usual, "oh, it's you" look and closed his eyes. I poured myself a glass of wine.

I was just refilling my glass when Margarito stomped onto the porch and rounded the corner into the kitchen. The rain was still coming down, hard. Neither of us said a word.

There was no way I could have driven out of Margarito's road in the mud that night. We took about an hour or two to wash up and rinse the mud from our clothes. Then we mopped up the mess on the floor. It was almost three in the morning when we finally went to bed.

It must have been five thirty, the sun was barely peeking over Sierra Rota, when a loud knocking woke me up. I was on a cot in the kitchen and closest to the door. I tried to get up. My head felt like it had been used for a bowling ball. My body refused to move. It had more or less gone all numb. I rolled over, fell off the cot, and landed on all fours. There was no way I could make it to the door.

More knocking. I pulled a blanket off the cot, covered myself and shouted, "Come in." That was a mistake. Bowling pins banged around in my head and I felt like I was going to upchuck.

The door burst open. It was Lario. He was obviously excited and held a rope in his hand. Actually, it was *the* rope. The thought came to me that he was there to hang us for rustling Maybelle. I groaned.

Lario stopped when he saw me. He looked at the less than half full jug on the table then looked back to me.

I couldn't raise my head. It was spinning around counterclockwise. Margarito shuffled into the kitchen from his room in the back of the house. Solo Vino came up to me and licked my face. That got me to my feet. Just for a moment. I fell right back down on the cot. At least I was sitting. Margarito pulled out a chair and sat at the table.

Lario's voice rang like a gunshot inside my head. "Somebody tried to steal Maybelle last night. I think I shot one of them. And they must have dropped this rope." He held it up. "I found it next to the house."

"Sh Maybelle aw right?" I managed to get out around my swollen tongue.

"Oh, yeah, she's all right, they didn't get her." Margarito hadn't said a word. I don't know how he did it but he got up and went to the stove, started a fire, and put on a pot of coffee.

Lario sat down at the table and tipped the jug of wine. "Jeez, you guys drank a lot of this stuff. Don't you know that junk can kill you?"

"Think it did," I mumbled.

Margarito shuffled back to the table and sat down. "What about tracks, did you find any?"

"No, the rain washed them out." Lario was obviously disappointed.

"What about the body of the guy you shot?"

"Nothing. I wanted to scare him and shot in the air. Maybe I just wounded him."

"Well, seems like he'll turn up sooner or later then." Margarito suggested. That seemed to settle Lario down.

I was feeling better by now, stood up and managed to pull three coffee cups from the trastero. Lario hung around long enough for the coffee to boil and to down a couple of cups. He felt better that no harm had been done and decided to buy a lock for Maybelle's corral gate.

For about a month after that Lario checked the weekly La Plaza paper for any news of the rustler he was sure he had shot. Margarito and I never spoke about that night and if it hadn't been for my torn jeans and shirt, I wouldn't even have been able to tell you for sure that the whole crazy thing had happened.

Margarito landed us a job making carved chairs and tables for a new restaurant in La Plaza. They wanted all the furnishings in a traditional style with wood pegs and Spanish-type carving on them. Eight tables and four chairs for each table kept the two of us pretty busy for most of the summer.

Lario was relieved that nobody had turned up in the emergency room to report a gunshot wound. Every time we'd stop by his house we made sure to check on Maybelle. Nothing seemed to have changed and I got to thinking the whole thing had been a waste of time. Finally, I asked Margarito about it. He assured me that Maybelle wouldn't start to show until she got pretty far along, maybe not even until she started to make a bag, because she was so fat.

Cows have pretty much the same gestation period as people, more or less nine months or 283 (or 5) days. I marked off the days the best I could remember on the calendar in the kitchen. Maybelle's due date looked like it was going to be pretty close to Easter. My grandmother got suspicious when she saw all my little red x's on her calendar and asked me if I'd gotten somebody pregnant. Of course I told her no, but I don't think she believed me. Maybelle wasn't a somebody, for god's sake, she was a cow. I didn't even have time for a date, let alone getting someone pregnant. All my time not spent gluing, sawing, carving, sanding, and varnishing chairs and tables was devoted to eating, sleeping, weeding the garden, fixing fences, cutting, hauling and splitting truckloads of firewood, or putting up hay for the winter.

Margarito and I barely finished the tables and chairs in time for the grand opening of the restaurant at Thanksgiving. There was even a story on page three of the La Plaza newspaper about the restaurant and the traditional "Spanish craftsmen from the little mountain community of Llano Alto" that made all the furniture. That brought us a few more orders for chairs and chests and the like that we had to complete before Christmas.

Margarito wasn't around much to help with the Christmas orders. He had to play his guitar and violin, like he did every year, for various school, church, and museum Christmas programs around the northern half of the state, and then there was Las Posadas. I delivered the final chair just three days before Christmas and had to tell the people not to let anyone sit in it until after Christmas because the varnish was still a little sticky. I gave them a five-dollar discount.

Winter finally settled in and life pretty much came to a screeching halt. Roads were periodically closed by snowstorms, fires and livestock needed to be fed, and most nights I was in bed by eight thirty. Two nights a week, either I went to Margarito's or he came over for my guitar lesson. We took our time finishing off Ted Archuleta's wine and by March there were still two or three glasses left in the jug. I stashed it in the tool shed behind my grandmother's house. We hadn't seen much of Lario or Alice except in church for Christmas and Día de los Santos Reyes on January sixth.

About two weeks before Easter, I saw a notice in Lebanon's store from our mayordomo setting a date to clean the ditch on the Saturday before Holy Week. On the appointed day Margarito, me, and most of the able-bodied men in the valley, shovels over our shoulders, lunches in paper sacks or beat-up lunch boxes, made the predawn trek to the headgate of the ditch.

That's where we saw Lario for the first time since Día de los Santos Reyes. He seemed to be pretty agitated about something. I figured that it was just because he'd been penned up all winter with Alice and the kids. I know I sure would have been a wreck.

That wasn't it.

Lario called Margarito and me aside. He couldn't stand still and he kept looking around to see if anybody could hear. "It's a milagro," he blurted. He kept shifting from one foot to the other.

I looked at Margarito. He looked at me and shook his head.

"What? A miracle?" we both said. Lario sure seemed to be upset. I was feeling sorry for the poor guy.

"It's Maybelle. She started making a bag two weeks ago. I think she's pregnant." His eyes had gone all wide and he made a little sign of the cross on his chest. Margarito and I just looked at each other. That's when the mayordomo gave the word to start.

Poor Lario. Margarito and I hadn't counted on how he would react to our date arranging stunt with Maybelle. To tell you the truth, I had pretty much accepted that nothing had come of it.

We worked along until about ten, when the mayordomo called a break. Margarito and I went looking for Lario. We found him surrounded by a group of men. His hands waved excitedly as he told them about the miraculous Maybelle pregnancy. Some of the men crossed themselves and nodded acknowledgment. After all, it was almost Semana Santa and stranger things had been known to happen. Others laughed and said that Maybelle was just fat. A couple of the guys said they had always known Lario was loco.

One of the men, Sosteno Pacheco, said that sometimes cows have false pregnancies and that she'd get over it in a while. Sosteno being the valley's ex oficio veterinarian and expert on all things bovine, equine, and ovine, that pretty much quieted things down. Lario told them all to go over and see for themselves.

And that's what happened. It seemed like no matter what they thought about Lario or Maybelle everyone wanted to see what was going on. We finished the whole two miles of ditch that afternoon with enough daylight left for everybody and their shovels to pile onto a handful of pickups and bounce over to see Lario's Maybelle milagro.

It had been a while since I'd seen Maybelle. Maybe it was because I knew something the others didn't but she sure looked to be in the motherly way to me.

The guys all just stood around offering suggestions about how it could have happened. They all knew that Maybelle had never been out of her corral. Or at least they all thought they knew.

"Maybe a bull got out from somewhere and jumped the fence."

"And then the bull just left?"

"Maybe Maybelle jumped the fence and found herself a bull."

"And then she just found her way home and let herself back in?"

"She's too fat to jump that fence."

"Maybe that's it. Maybe she's just fat."

"Maybe it's like Sosteno said, false pregnancy."

Sosteno climbed over the log rails of the corral and strode over to Maybelle. Maybelle turned her head, looked at him, and went back to chewing her cud, unconcerned. Everybody got all quiet. Sosteno lifted Maybelle's tail and looked. He felt her udder. He pulled softly on a teat. He put his hands against her belly and pushed. He looked in her mouth and ran his hands along her neck and back. We all just stood there, waiting for the verdict.

Sosteno was enjoying the attention. He took his time and had this expression on his face like he was being all thoughtful. He slowly walked back across the corral and started over the log rails. When he got to the top rail he sat there and looked back over his shoulder at Maybelle. You could have heard grass grow, it was that quiet.

I have to admit, he could sure put on a show.

Finally, he said it. "She's pregnant. Any day now."

A shriek came from behind us. We all jumped about two feet and turned around. Alice had come out of the house just in time for pronouncement of Sosteno's verdict.

She had fainted dead away.

Lario ran to Alice, picked her up, and carried her into the house.

Margarito and I just looked at each other. Nobody said anything but I knew word of the "Maybelle milagro" would be all over half the state by midnight. Everybody left after that.

Margarito and I retrieved our shovels from a pickup and went in the house to check on Alice. She was sitting up on the couch, rosary in her hand, reciting Hail Marys as fast as her lips could move. Lario was sitting there beside her. He really looked worried. I was beginning to feel pretty bad about the whole thing and thought maybe I should tell them what had really happened. But then I remembered how close that bullet had come to perforating my head in the middle of the night during a pouring rain. I didn't think he'd stand a chance of missing me this time.

Once we were pretty sure Alice would be all right, Margarito and I started home on foot. We were unusually silent and parted with plans to clean his lateral ditches in the morning. It was dark by the time I got home, put up the shovel, tossed hay to the sheep, fed the dogs, and wandered into the kitchen looking for dinner. My grandmother was on the telephone. She was talking excitedly in Spanish and I picked up a few words like Lario, Alice, vaca, Maybelle, embarazada, and milagro. She hadn't even started dinner.

By the time I'd washed up and heated some three-day-old beans, tortillas, and leftover lamb ribs, she had answered the phone two more times. It was the same thing, over and over, all evening long. As soon as she hung up the phone, it would ring again. I finished eating and left a plateful of food for her on the table, went to my room and practiced my guitar for a while but my heart wasn't in it. I finally fell asleep.

I woke up in the morning to the telephone's ring and the sound of cars going by on the road, headed in the direction of Lario and Alice's house. My grandmother was on the telephone again so I went out, grabbed my shovel, and walked over to Margarito's. He was standing on the porch when I showed up, sipping a cup of coffee and watching the line of cars snaking down from the llano toward Lario and Alice's. He looked at me and grinned. I couldn't help it, I just started laughing.

We worked on his ditches and got them in pretty good shape by lunchtime. After lunch we figured that we might as well go over to Lario's and see how Alice was doing. I was pretty worried about her and Lario and the kids. We decided to walk since the traffic was so heavy. Margarito said he'd never seen anything like it.

It turned out that we had been worried for nothing.

The yard and corrals were full of people. The oldest kid, I think his name is Roger, had opened a gate in the pasture across the road from the house and was charging twenty-five cents per car for parking. A steady stream of people filed from the pasture parking lot to Maybelle's corral and back. A couple of the younger kids were busy selling lemonade, Kool-Aid, and some kind of cards from a hastily made board-on-cinder-blocks stand.

The logs of Maybelle's corral were draped with rosaries, handwritten pleas for one blessing or another, holy cards with pictures of saints, milagros, and a few card things that I didn't recognize.

Good old Maybelle, she seemed to take it all in stride. Lario had brushed her until her coat shone, made sure she had plenty of hay, and roped off a part of the corral so people wouldn't be able to touch her. I'm sure her udder was twice as big as it had been yesterday. She looked like her delivery day was getting pretty close.

Lario was all dressed up in his cleanest jeans and pearl-button black Western shirt acting like an usher, helping people file past Maybelle's humble little shed. His Elvis-style haircut and muttonchop sideburns glistened in the sunlight. Along the edges of the corral there must have been a half dozen people on their knees, rosaries in hand, praying in unison. I was a little overwhelmed by it all. I think Margarito might have been too. I followed him into the house.

Alice was there. She was busy directing a whole tribe of nieces and nephews. The kids were all strung out in a loosely organized assembly line making hand-drawn colored-pencil cards of a smiling cow with a halo over her head. I recognized them as the cards that had been stuck all over the logs of the corral. One of the kids that had been out at the lemonade stand, I think it was Simon, came in and dropped what must have been ten pounds of change on the kitchen table. He grabbed a stack of cards and ran back outside. Alice ran over to us, gave us a hug and one each of the haloed smiling Maybelle cards.

It looked like Alice and Lario had gotten over the shock of the Maybelle milagro and were doing pretty good. Margarito and I left. We had work to do.

We spent the rest of the afternoon cleaning the little lateral ditches that fed my grandmother's orchard and garden and raking up winter's debris. The traffic going by on the road just got more and more heavy all afternoon long. By the time we finished up, the phone had pretty much stopped ringing and Grandma called us in for dinner.

We went in to a meal of papitas, roasted whole green chiles, and sliced beef. We ate in silence. I guess we were all hungry.

After dinner I remembered the haloed Maybelle holy card that I had stuck in my jacket pocket. I set it on the table in front of my grandmother. She didn't even look at it.

"So, Ricardo, what did you do?"

"I don't know, Grandma. What are you talking about?"

"And you, Margarito, were you a part of all this?"

Margarito and I just looked at each other.

She sighed, got up from her chair and walked over to the calendar where I had marked off the days of Maybelle's pregnancy. I felt a chill run up and down my spine. Margarito hung his head and looked at me from the corner of his eye. I think he was smiling. Maybe it was a grimace.

"According to this, Maybelle should have her calf on Good Friday," my grandmother pronounced. She turned around and grinned. "Let's see if my grandson can count. That would be a real milagro."

"You're not mad?"

"No."

"You're not going to tell?"

"What? Are you loco? I haven't had this much fun since . . . I don't know how long it's been. Today, I talked to people I haven't seen for twenty years. Some are even going to come visit. Llano Alto hasn't had this much excitement since the Pueblo Revolt. And even better, you gave people something to believe in. Not to mention Lario and Alice will make enough money from all this to buy new clothes for the kids, and a washing machine for Alice, maybe even a clothes dryer. Now, go get that wine from the shed where you thought you hid it and let's have a glass to celebrate."

Darn, she was good.

By Wednesday, the line of cars going to Lario and Alice's was bumper to bumper. It wound back over the llano and through the plaza. Neighbors along the way opened pastures and started charging for parking too. There got to be a whole lot of people just walking the last quarter mile or so to Maybelle's corral. The assembly line of kids was doing its best to crank out Maybelle cards but it seemed like they were falling behind. Even with Margarito's help.

I offered to take a roughed-out, uncolored sample to a copy place in La Plaza and run off a few hundred copies, if I could get out onto the road through all the traffic. Alice handed me a heavy sack of change and a piece of paper with four line-drawn Maybelles on it.

"Ricardo," Alice called as I hurried out the door. "More lemonade and Kool-Aid, ice too. And more colored pencils." I waved my hand in the air and took off on my mission.

I couldn't get out to the road so I drove around the back way, through an arroyo, over an old logging road that topped out on the far end of the llano, back down through the Río del Indio, into Río Pueblo, and took off to La Plaza. I'd already lost half an hour.

I don't know when I'd seen the like of the traffic that was converging on the valley. Cars and trucks were coming from all directions. It looked like I might need to make more than a couple hundred copies of haloed Maybelle holy cards.

The copy place was on a little side street off the plaza. I pulled up and wandered in with my Maybelle line drawings and sack of coins. Nobody paid any attention to me. The two girls behind the counter had their eyes glued to a TV.

There on the screen were Maybelle and a beaming Lario and Alice and all the kids. The commentator, I don't know his name because my grandmother and I still didn't have a TV, was going on, all excited, about the Semana Santa miracle of the pregnant cow in Llano Alto. I snuck a little closer so I could hear what he was saying. "Is it an immaculate conception or an immaculate deception?" A big banner popped up on the screen, "HOLY COW?" I dropped the sack of change.

One of the girls turned around and "ssshh'd" me. She held up a finger. I guessed it meant I should wait for a minute.

"... To the faithful it really doesn't matter..." The picture switched to show the line of cars and trucks filing through the Llano Alto plaza and down the road to Lario and Alice's house.

"... People have flocked to the tiny mountain community of Llano Alto to catch a glimpse of the cow that got pregnant without the benefit of a bull." Another banner popped up on the TV screen, "NO BULL!"

I bent down to pick up the coins that had spilled out when I dropped the sack.

When I stood back up the girl that "shh'd" me was leaning over the counter. "Can I help you?"

There was some priest on the TV screen now talking about how the church had a whole bunch of investigator priests whose special job it was to look into reported miracles and how in cases like this, the Church's official position was particularly skeptical, or something like that. I slid the sheet of Maybelle drawings across the counter to her. She looked at it. She looked at me.

"Uhh, it's for them, Lario and Alice." I pointed to the TV. "They couldn't leave."

She smiled then. "How many copies?"

We calculated that a thousand Maybelles would be two hundred fifty pages, at five cents a copy. I got busy counting out coins while she started running off the copies. It seemed like a lot but judging from the number of vehicles I'd seen heading to Llano Alto and if my cow gestation calendar was right we might need even more.

The TV fellow was trying to make some sort of comparison between all the people going to see Maybelle and the annual pilgrimage to the Santuarío, in Chimayo. It seemed to me like he was more or less milking the story for everything he could get out of it. I still had a lot of change left so I asked her to run me another hundred pages just to be sure.

I paid up, left each of the girls a sheet of haloed Maybelles for their trouble, and headed off to get the Kool-Aid, lemonade, ice, and colored pencils. By the time I got back to Río Pueblo the line of cars had crossed the llano and wound its way down into the valley. I gunned my truck and went around the back road. The same way I'd come. A handful of vehicles saw me and started following. Pretty soon I could see in my rearview mirror a whole line of cars and pickups winding through my dust. The cars all had to drop out when I drove through the Río Del Indio and started up the back road.

I made it to the house with everything intact, except the ice had about one-fourth melted. A couple that had followed me in their truck helped carry the bags of melting ice into the house. They were nice and had driven all the way from Santa Fe. They were supposed to meet up in Llano Alto with some friends from Albuquerque. Alice put them to work with scissors quartering up Maybelle pages.

It seemed like half the kids in Llano Alto and some from Río Pueblo were crowded into every room of the house coloring and cutting out Maybelle cards. It didn't seem to matter what colors they used, the cards were flying out the door in stacks and buckets of coins were being drug back in by grinning kids that had figured out they could wander up and down the line of cars selling the things.

I went out and looked around for Margarito. I didn't find him. No wonder. The whole place had turned into a city. Down by the river, people were pitching tents. I guessed they intended to keep a vigil until Maybelle had her calf. Across the road a Channel Seven TV news truck had set up shop and people were lined up six deep waiting to be interviewed.

A few local families had set up stands and were selling food and drinks to the pilgrims. It looked like more people than just Lario and Alice were going to benefit from all the hoopla. I guess that was a good thing after all.

I went home. It took me most of a half hour to negotiate the way back in my truck. Little groups of people had abandoned their cars at different points along the road or had parked in the plaza or a neighbor's pasture and were walking to the scene of the impending calving. One group would pass me and I'd scoot ahead about twenty feet to the next group. It was like that until I finally turned off to my grandmother's.

Toward dark, things had quieted down. People left for home or went to motels in La Plaza or wherever. Groups of people, guided by local kids, still shuffled by on foot, their way lit by flashlights. The traffic had slowed a lot but it was still more than we were used to.

My grandmother and I sat on the porch enjoying the evening breeze and the last of the chokecherry wine. The really amazing thing to me was how nobody had gotten mad at the slow-moving traffic, nobody honked their horns, nobody had gotten in a fight. I hadn't heard a harsh word all day. I drained the last of the wine and suddenly felt very tired.

The next morning, I left early. My grandmother was expecting some friends of hers to show up from Santa Fe, Dos Cabezas, Las Vegas, and Albuquerque. It wasn't that I minded a houseful of guests, I just wasn't looking forward to another day of not being able to get out when I wanted to. She asked me to pick up a few grocery things at Lebanon's.

I drove over to Margarito's. He wasn't home. I guess he was still helping out at Lario and Alice's. I filled Solo's food bowl, threw the sheep some hay, made sure they had water, and then drove down to Río Pueblo. I swung by Roberto's Café for a cup of coffee.

The place was full and of course the talk was all about Maybelle. Roberto and Lucia were turning out the house specialty, red chile huevos rancheros, as fast as they could and I figured they would probably set some sort of sales record. They even had a couple local high school girls working as waitresses.

The only person in the place I recognized was Sosteno Pacheco. He was sitting in the last booth, nursing a cup of coffee and talking to a guy who was taking notes. Sosteno looked up and nodded to me. I nodded back and downed my coffee. A Channel Four news truck pulled up outside. I paid and went out the back door as the news crew marched into the café with a video camera and microphones. Roberto headed me off just as I was getting on my truck and asked if I'd pick up a dozen packages of tortillas, a case of eggs, and some other things from Lebanon's. "Just put them on my bill," he instructed.

I guess, knowing the truth, I couldn't get too excited about the whole thing. It amazed me how it had grown into such a ginormous deal. At least my friends and neighbors were making some money off it and I was glad that people had found something festive to focus on.

I don't think the Church was too happy about it, after all it was Semana Santa, but I figured they would survive. By this time next year, it would be hard to find anyone who even remembered Maybelle. I cruised up to Lebanon's.

It was hard to find a parking place. I looked up the road to Lynch's. It was the same. I drove around behind Lebanon's and walked in through the delivery door. About that time the newspapers arrived from Santa Fe and La Plaza. Darned if the story about Maybelle hadn't made the headlines. I bought a copy of each for me, Margarito, and Lario and Alice. Lebanon was busy with customers so I wheeled my little cart around the store, bought the stuff for Roberto and my grandmother, and beat it out to my truck.

I sat there reading the stories, *La Plaza News* first. It seemed to me the writer had gotten a little carried away. He'd borrowed a line from the newscast I'd seen at the copy shop. "HOLY COW" was splashed across the front page and the story ran over to page three. The writer managed to stretch parallels with everything from San Isidro Labrador to Hindu sacred cows. He wrapped it up with a reference to traditional Spanish-American herdsmen and the "culture of livestock" that had predominated in the West ever since the Spanish conquistadores. He even brought in some references to vaqueros, and their influence on American popular culture. I wasn't too sure about all that but it was a pretty piece of creative writing and next to it were all the usual stories about Easter, traditional observances, rebirth, Spring, and the like.

The Santa Fe paper wasn't quite as nice. They'd picked up on the "immaculate deception" theme and spent a lot of ink on interviews with different priests and preachers that took issue with people spending Holy Week driving up to the mountains to look at a pregnant cow instead of being in church. It was about what I'd expected. The writer, an Anglo, went off on a discussion about how New Mexicans were always looking for hidden religious meanings in unusual occurrences like saints in window glass or Jesus's face on an adobe wall. He even made a reference about the annual Semana Santa pilgrimage to the Santuarío in Chimayo. I figured the writer and editor would be looking for new jobs by next week.

I dropped off the eggs, tortillas, and other stuff at Roberto's with a copy of the bill and drove home. My grandmother wasn't there when I finally made it back and I guessed she and her friends had gone over to see Maybelle. I figured I might as well do the same.

Good Friday morning finally came. It was appropriately dark and heavily overcast. My grandmother and her friends got ready to go to church in Río Pueblo. I walked over to Lario's. No calf.

It seemed like the excitement was beginning to wear off. Either that or a lot people were in church, which was more or less to be expected. The Hermanos had shut themselves in their morada and I guess when it came right down to it people were going to do what they always did, regardless of how many miracles might be happening around them. It was a good thing though that it had quieted down. Lario, Alice, and the kids were worn out.

Noon came and still no calf. Silence settled over the valley. The mood over at Lario and Alice's wasn't much different. People were just hanging around, munching on apples and tortillas, washing them down with Kool-Aid, and speculating on when the calf was going to make its appearance. It started to snow. People started to leave.

Margarito and I were just sitting there under Lario's apricot tree. The snow was getting heavier and sticking to the ground. More people left. The news truck people started packing things up.

"How long does it take for a miracle to happen?" I asked Margarito, half serious, half joking. Actually, I was becoming concerned for Maybelle's welfare.

He just looked at me for a minute. "I think maybe, the miracle has already happened." He finally said.

I thought about that and finally said, "Which miracle do you mean?"

"Well, just think about how Ted Archuleta didn't have enough money to pay us and gave us that jug of chokecherry wine."

"Uh huh." I still didn't feel like we were on the same page.

"And think how Maybelle was in heat, and how it started raining, and Juan Trujillo happened to have a bull."

I thought I was beginning to see where this was going. "And how Lario didn't perforate me with his .30-30," I contributed.

"That's a good point. Actually, that's a really good point. Lario never misses. And how the rain washed out our tracks."

I was sort of on a miracle roll now. "I was thinking the other day how all those people came from all over the state to see Maybelle and nothing bad happened. No fights, no honking, no pushing or shoving, no mean words."

"See? That's what I mean." His eyes sparkled. "It's all a series of little day to day miracles, one after the other, that add up to the one big miracle of life."

I thought about that for a minute or two. There I'd been, living right in the middle of a whole bunch of miracles, and I hadn't even seen it because I'd been waiting for the big one to come around. I shivered. Snow slipped down the collar of my jacket. The news truck left, followed by the last straggler pickups. It suddenly got so quiet you could hear snowflakes floating past in the air and striking the branches overhead.

Margarito stood and stamped his feet. "We better go, this is going to be a big one."

Lario called at first light to let us know that in the night, during the storm, Maybelle had given birth to a shiny red heifer calf. The kids had already named her "Stormy."

No one had been there to see it happen except a couple billion pure white snowflakes.

TÍO MELECIO

IT HAD RAINED LAST NIGHT. One of those late October storms that come in gusty bursts, briefly let up, then come back around with more of the same. Fits of wind rattled skeletal tree branches. Summer's spent leaves, blown by the wind, rustled an insistent warning, against windows and doors, of the coming winter.

The mountains to the east had hidden all day behind a gray shroud of low-hanging clouds. There was no doubt they had received a fresh coating of snow. The ground was still muddy and would be frozen with a thin crust tomorrow morning.

The wind carried the scent of winter. Men would be huddled over hot coffee making predictions when the first snow would close the road to La Plaza, recalling past winters' storms and hard times. Secretly, they speculated as to how many more trips they could make into the high country for firewood.

Margarito hadn't been feeling well lately and I decided to stop by his place on my way home from work. I awkwardly hugged an oversized white Styrofoam cup of red chile and a couple paper-wrapped tortillas under my coat, to keep them warm. A three-day-thick lump of mail I had pried from Margarito's overstuffed mailbox and a couple magazines I had picked up for him in La Plaza threatened to slip from my hand. His sheep, closed in their corral for the night, bleated a soft greeting around mouthfuls of hay.

I stomped my feet as I made my way along the front portal to the kitchen door. Margarito would hear me coming and some of the mud that clung to my boots would be knocked free.

A burst of superheated air greeted me as I stepped through the turquoise door into the kitchen. No Margarito.

The blue enamel coffee pot was spewing steam and coffee grounds from its spout onto the stove top where they burned, giving off an acrid and bitter odor. Bessie, the huge wood-burning cookstove, glowed a deep threatening red. I tossed the mail on the table and delivered the chile and tortillas from the womb of my jacket beside it.

I closed the stove vent a little to head off a meltdown and moved the coffeepot off to the cooler side of the stove. I dug a plastic spoon from the linty depths of my jacket pocket, retrieved the chile, tortillas, stack of mail, and magazines, and shuffled toward the bedroom at the back of the L-shaped adobe.

I found Margarito sitting in bed under a mound of blankets and quilts that must have been a foot deep. His guitar and violin, never far from his hand, leaned against a wall, within easy reach. A haphazard stack of well-read magazines balanced precariously close to the edge of a chair doing double duty as a bedside table. One of the magazines had slid onto the floor.

Across the room, a tiny black-and-white television, displaying some long-legged blond woman turning squares, sat lopsided on a chair. The volume was so low that I could hear only an occasional dinging. Solo Vino, lying on the floor at the foot of the bed, lifted one shaggy-browed eye in my direction and immediately let out an "oh, it's just you" sigh.

"From Lario," Margarito muttered, glancing toward the TV. "I guess he thought I needed the company."

I tossed the mail and magazines onto the pile of blankets in the area of what looked like it might be his lap and turned toward a chair in the corner. I slid the chair with my foot closer to the bed, balancing the Styrofoam cup, tortillas, and spoon in my hands.

"Brought you some chile and tortillas from Roberto's."

"Good, I don't feel much like cooking." Margarito laughed and shivered despite the pile of blankets and the superheated room. Nothing can hold the heat like an old adobe.

"Have you seen a doctor?" I asked.

"No, I'm a lot better." He answered a little too quickly.

"I must have missed the funeral." I tried to sound serious. He laughed. The shadow of a cough made its way up and I immediately felt better. At least it wasn't into his lungs.

"You want the chile?" He nodded eagerly as he absently poked through the stack of mail.

I stuck the spoon into the cup, handed the chile and tortillas to him, then slid my jacket off, onto the chair back. "Coffee?" I asked. He nodded and I walked back to the kitchen.

By the time I returned to the bedroom with two cups of steaming, still bubbling coffee that looked and stunk like superheated volcanic mud, he had finished off the chile and both tortillas. The cup and spoon had joined the stack of magazines on the chair next to the bed. I balanced a yellow coffee cup on the bedcovers within reach of his hand and kept the lime green one for myself.

"You know," he said slowly, "I've had a lot of time to think about things while I've been sick."

"Uh huh." I tried to show him that I was interested in spite of the hot cup burning the skin off my left palm.

"I turned down the stove a little," I informed him. "And I'll bring in some wood before I leave." He nodded and slid a little deeper under the covers. The yellow cup, carefully steadied by one finger, tottered on the edge of the bed.

"Roberto makes the best chile in the valley," Margarito commented. "That was really good."

He continued thoughtfully. "I used to have an uncle named Melecio Rael. He was married to my uncle's wife's sister, Nefe."

I nodded as if I knew his family tree as well as my own and blew on my coffee. It had stopped bubbling but I was still too intimidated to bring it to my lips.

"I don't know why I was thinking of him. Maybe because I thought I was going to die from this stinking flu. I've been thinking about a lot of things these past few days."

I nodded that I understood. I had done that myself, a time or two.

"Melecio was more or less a scoundrel. Actually, more than less. He was a little guy, maybe five foot three. He and his family used to live up the road in that old house next to Prudencio Ortega. It seemed like he was always doing some stupid thing to try and get rich quick. The problem was, he never did get rich and he sure wasn't very honest. He wasn't very smart either. It seemed like someone with blood in their eye was always hunting for him. I was pretty young so I don't remember too much of what he did." He hesitated for a moment, thinking.

"I remember one time he sold a piece of land that didn't belong to him to some brothers from La Plaza. That cost him his front teeth. Then, he was selling shares in a nonexistent gold mine in the mountains. I think someone broke his arm over that one, or maybe that was what cost him the rest of his teeth. Maybe it was a broken leg . . . I just don't remember for sure. You could hardly understand him when he talked because he didn't have any teeth. All us kids thought it was pretty funny, the way he talked.

"Then there was the time he got caught with a trailer load of Esteban Trujillo's cattle. That one nearly got him killed. But Esteban was Melecio's sister's father-in-law, or something like that, and she wouldn't let the old man shoot him. She took care of it in her own way. She whacked Melecio with a cast iron frying pan and wouldn't let him back in the house. I remember that he had a pretty big scar over his left eye from where she hit him."

Margarito raised the yellow cup and glanced suspiciously at the contents. He gently set it back on the quilt.

"It seemed like every time I'd see him, he had another scar somewhere, or was missing something, like a finger or his teeth. Or he had one arm or the other in a cast or a sling. He even lost an eye somehow. He got where he looked pretty used up and he lost a lot of weight because he didn't have any teeth and couldn't eat much. But he always had some kind of plan about how he was going to get rich. I used to think he was pretty exciting. But I was young and didn't know much.

"Anyway, I was thinking about him the other day for some reason. I still remember how we hadn't seen him for about twenty years. Then we heard that he got killed in Albuquerque. Maybe it was Denver."

"No," I blurted. "For reals?"

"Well yeah, of course. It was just a matter of time before somebody finally caught up with him. I don't know how it took so long.

"We never did hear the whole story about what happened. Just that he was shot or stabbed. Maybe both. After that, I saw my tía Nefe a couple times for the fiestas but then I didn't see her any more either. She might have gone to California with a new husband."

"Somebody must have wanted him pretty bad." I felt a little silly, stating the obvious.

Margarito nodded, "Yeah, we never did hear who killed him. It could have been anybody . . . or at least half the people in the state. But still, for some reason, what I was thinking about was the time he tried to steal from the priest."

I gave up trying to hold onto the cup and set it on the floor, in the middle of a red and yellow flower pattern in the linoleum.

"The priest?" I couldn't imagine what anyone would steal from a priest. "You mean from the church?"

Margarito attempted a sip of the coffee. He gave up too and set his cup on the chair next to the bed. He slid up a little from under the covers. I reached over and moved the stack of mail to where I thought it wouldn't end up on the floor.

"No, the priest. At that time, we had a priest in Río Pueblo who had been married before he was ordained. He came from somewhere like Socorro or Magdalena, maybe Deming. Anyway, wherever it was, there were a lot of rumors about him."

I nodded. Nobody in the valley was safe from rumors. Somehow, if anything happened, to anybody, everybody in town knew about it and swore they were telling the truth because they had heard it from someone who had heard it from someone who had seen everything.

"Some people said the priest had children that he abandoned, others said he had killed his wife and became a priest for penance. That never made much sense to me, but who knows?

"Some people were more kind and told stories about how he had given his life to God after his wife died from a long illness, or in some kind of accident.

"Somehow, Melecio became obsessed with the idea that the priest was rich and had a cache of jewels or gold or whatever, that he carried around with him so nobody could steal it. Where the priest could have kept such a treasure I don't know. My friends and I used to sit in church and try to figure out how much treasure he could be hiding under the vestments he wore at mass.

"To make things worse, that priest always wore a gold ring with a big red gem of some kind. Maybe it was a ruby. Maybe it was glass. Nobody really knew. It didn't matter to Melecio. He suddenly started going to Mass every Sunday, something he hadn't done in years. The family all thought their prayers had been answered and that he had finally realized the error of his ways.

"I remember how Melecio's eye followed that ring everywhere. Every move the ring made during Mass was matched by his wandering eye. When the priest raised the host overhead, Melecio's eye looked toward heaven. When the priest stood outside the church after mass and greeted people as they left the church, he would shake their hands. Melecio's head bobbed up and down with every move of the ring. It seemed like he went out of his way to shake hands with the priest whenever he saw him just so he could touch that ring. He even volunteered to help with plastering the church."

Margarito slid the coffee cup into his hand and managed a noisy sip of the stuff. He made a face almost as bitter as the brown, barely liquid contents of the cup. I glanced at my lime green cup in the middle of the red and yellow flower and decided to give it a little more time to cool. I even considered the sacrilege of going to the kitchen for some sugar.

Margarito shifted under the quilt mound. I lurched forward and caught the mail as it avalanched toward the floor. I tossed the errant letters and magazines onto the other side of the bed and settled back on one cheek with my arm over the back of the chair. Solo Vino released a prolonged, irritated sigh and shifted his position.

"Nobody could have guessed where this was all going to lead. Everyone in Melecio's house seemed to be just holding their breath, waiting to see how long he could keep himself out of trouble. It seemed like he kept up his good behavior for about three or four months, I don't remember exactly. And, it seemed like maybe he had changed for good. Nobody could have guessed the great sin Melecio would commit before it was all over."

Margarito glanced toward the television and then toward his cup. "That stuff tastes like crap."

I thought he was probably right and decided my cup looked pretty good right where it was.

"It seems like God had other plans though." He stopped just like that and looked at me for a moment. Some ad jingle was playing on the television.

"So? What happened?" I urged, flapping my hand impatiently. My butt had gone numb and I shifted to the other cheek.

A stray gust of wind raced down the valley and whistled under the eaves of the house. Dead, dry leaves and a few heavy drops of rain rattled against the windows. Solo grumbled a complaint, stretched and rolled onto his back, feet in the air. I suddenly felt a chill and glanced toward the windows. A very dark night had settled over the valley beneath the overcast sky.

Margarito's eyes smiled. "The priest died."

I straightened in the chair. "Are you telling me Melecio killed the priest?"

"No, nothing like that. He died right there in front of everybody at Mass. It was probably a heart attack or a massive stroke, something like that," Margarito explained.

"One minute he was raising the host over his head, the next he was just lying there, dead. You could hear this huge sucking sound as everyone in the church drew in their breath and the rustle of clothing as they hurried to cross themselves. Then it got real quiet, and everybody just stayed there kneeling. I looked at the lady next to me. I remember her eyes were big round circles of fear. Everyone was frozen and time stood still. I can only guess what Melecio was thinking. Then, after a few minutes everybody exhaled in a loud whoosh and some of the men rushed toward the altar, Melecio in the lead.

"One lady up front fainted and the people near her must have jumped about five feet before they realized she was still breathing. Someone sat her up and fanned her with their hands. Somebody else brought a handful of holy water from the font that they threw in her face.

"It was official, the priest was declared dead. Nobody seemed to know what to do. After some discussion they carried the body into the vestry at the side of the church. He was a pretty big man and it took four men to carry him. Some of the women followed and knelt down with rosaries in their hands to watch over the body. Melecio hovered like an expectant father whose wife was in childbirth.

"In those days we were pretty isolated up here. No paved roads and only a couple telephones at the stores. Everybody would go there, to the stores, to call their relatives in Albuquerque or Santa Fe. Somebody, I don't remember who, went to call the archbishop in Santa Fe.

"By then, the rest of the people came to their senses. We were all standing around in the church, huddled in little groups of four or five. The stories were already boiling over the pot. Someone claimed that they had seen a bolt of lightning strike the priest. Another person said that they had seen a hand take form out of the air and tap the priest on the chest just before he collapsed. Somebody else said they had smelled burning sulfur just before it happened. I felt sort of left out because I hadn't seen or smelled anything.

"Whoever it was that had gone to call Santa Fe returned after a little while. The archbishop was somewhere between Las Cruces and Santa Fe. Nobody knew how to get hold of him. Nobody knew what to do. After a lot of discussion, Melecio suggested that we should right away go ahead and bury the priest. He reminded us that it was July and there was no way to preserve the body until we heard from the archbishop. If the archbishop wanted to move the body later, he could. Los Hermanos could perform the required duties and say the prayers. Everybody agreed with Melecio.

"Melecio stepped up then and took charge, giving orders to everyone. He sent some of the men to put together a coffin. He ordered others to get shovels from their trucks and wagons and they set about digging a grave in the churchyard. The burial would take place the next morning. All of us left for home, except the three or four women that stayed to pray with the body. I was curious so I snuck out of the house and went to the church to watch what would happen next.

"Melecio and a couple men returned to the church with water and towels. The body was washed, dressed in the priest's cleanest black robe and placed in the simple pine board coffin before dark arrived.

Nobody found any treasure in a belt. Or anywhere else. The men told Melecio what a good job he had done of organizing everything. Melecio was grinning like a kid on Christmas morning. The men and Melecio left. By then it was nearly dark and I went home."

Margarito stopped for a moment, thinking, remembering.

I reached for my coffee and took a sip. It wasn't any better cold than it had promised to be when hot and I spit it back into the cup. Margarito laughed at my expression and suggested that I get a couple beers from the refrigerator. I gathered both cups, hurried to the kitchen, poured the vile liquid down the sink, tossed three or four pieces of wood in the firebox, grabbed and opened a couple beers, and returned to my chair. I handed one of the cold beers to Margarito. We let out sighs of relief in unison as the beer went down.

By then, Margarito was ready to continue. "Sometime during the night, close to morning, Melecio must have returned to the church. He was all sympathy for the women who had stayed behind to pray and watch the body. He had a rosary in one hand and a Bible in the other. He insisted that the women should go home since they would have to get up in a couple hours for the funeral. He would stay and keep watch. They admitted that they were pretty tired. Melecio went right to his knees and started reciting the rosary, his eye on the heavens. The women left him alone with the priest's body.

"I guess one of the women began to feel guilty about leaving Melecio alone. She woke her husband and son and convinced them to go to the church and sit with him and the priest's corpse. The men hurried to the church and entered the vestry. No Melecio. They looked all around, inside and outside of the church, calling him. He was nowhere to be found. They thought he must have gone to answer a call of nature or maybe he had gotten scared being there by himself and gone home.

"The father and son spent the rest of the night watching over the body, reciting the rosary and saying the prayers for the dead. They had no idea that Melecio was there, in the room with them, quietly saying prayers of his own. For once, he was sincere, praying that no one would think to check the lid of the hastily built coffin.

"You see, he hadn't expected anyone to return to the church. He must have pried the lid off the coffin and was trying to remove the gold and ruby ring from the priest's finger. Rigor mortis had probably set in and try as he might, he couldn't slip the ring from the finger. He pulled out his pocket knife and was in the process of cutting off the finger when the man and his son returned to the church. Just as he heard their footsteps coming, the finger came loose, slipped from his hand, and fell into the coffin. Melecio wasn't about to let the fortune, that he had held so briefly, escape. Without a moment's hesitation he threw himself into the coffin with the corpse and pulled the lid over them, just as the men entered the vestry."

"Holy crap!"

"I know. What it must have been like in there, I sure wouldn't want to know. But . . . Melecio was Melecio.

"Sunrise came and the people all gathered for the priest's funeral. Still no Melecio. Nefe hadn't seen him. The men decided that they would finish the burial as quickly as possible and organize a search party for him.

"All the people gathered around the freshly dug grave. I think there were about twenty or thirty of us. In those days we still had professional mourners. I remember how they wailed and prayed beside the grave. They were all dressed in long black dresses with black shawls over their heads and ashes smeared on their faces. People were crowded around all close to the grave as the coffin was carried out of the church. The Hermanos followed along singing their alabados and despedidas. In their haste, none of the pallbearers seemed to notice the extra weight or check the fit of the lid."

Margarito stopped and took another sip of beer. I did too.

"I still remember what happened next, like it was yesterday. My little sister, Guadalupe, was standing in front of our mother at the foot of the grave. I was standing a little behind them and to the left of my mother so I could see. The men prayed and sang as they carried the coffin and set it on the thick ropes that would be used to lower it to rest, however temporary. The mourners wailed.

"The pallbearers shuffled along the sides of the grave. They held the ropes tightly in their twelve hands, straining against the weight of the coffin and its occupants. They started to lower the coffin.

"Melecio must have realized that he was about to be buried alive. Suddenly, a piercing wail that drowned out even the mourners rose from the coffin. The men holding the ropes jumped back. They let go of the ropes.

"The coffin dropped straight down into the grave, feet first. The lid came flying off and Melecio came flying out, shrieking like a wild-eyed fury from hell, arms waving and thrashing. Everyone turned and fled. People crossed themselves as they ran, calling on God to save them.

"I ran about twenty yards and was nearly the last person in the headlong exodus when I realized that I didn't see Guadalupe. I could hear her screaming, all hysterical, and ran back to help her. I was always brave when it came to my little sister and would have done battle with a demon, even Lucifer himself to save her. Somehow, Guadalupe had been pushed in the panic and fell into the grave.

"That's when I saw Melecio. He scrambled up from the depths like a scalded spider and ran off, away from everyone else. He knew that I saw him, and I never saw him again. I reached over the edge and pulled Guadalupe from the grave. She was shaking with the terror of it all and I held her tightly in my arms. Lying in the loose soil, at the bottom of the grave, was the priest's finger with the gold and red ring.

"Our mother suddenly realized that neither I nor Guadalupe were anywhere to be found. She and a couple of her brothers returned to the grave a few minutes later. Guadalupe had stopped screaming but she was still shaking badly and mother took us home.

"Some men got the priest and his bejeweled finger buried after all and eventually the archbishop came and performed a proper funeral mass. The priest's family came to the mass and they decided to leave him buried in the churchyard. His headstone is still there today.

"But the really interesting part was how nobody realized it was Melecio that came flying out of that coffin. That evening, I overheard the men talking about the demonio that had almost been buried in sacred ground and flew, shrieking, out of the priest's coffin. Nobody could quite explain the finger until Donciano Ortiz suggested that the demon might have been trying to steal the ring and suddenly realized that it was about to be placed in sacred ground. In its haste to be free of the coffin the demon must have dropped the finger, just before it had vanished into thin air.

"That's the way it was told for years around the mountains and everyone seemed to be satisfied with that. I never told them how close to the truth they really were."

FLORIAN CISNEROS

THERE WAS THIS GUY. I'd see him every once in a while, at Lebanon's or Lynch's stores, sometimes at a gas station. His skin was the deeply etched farmer/rancher walnut of people who spent most of their lives outdoors. His scuffed boots, patched Lee blue jeans and sun-faded shirts with barbed wire tears in them were pretty much the same as everybody else's in the valley. What got my attention was the jagged scar on his face. And the way people reacted whenever he showed up.

Everybody was nice enough to him and he was real friendly but I couldn't help noticing that whenever he walked into a store, everybody in the place would make a discreet little sign of the cross on their forehead, lips, or chest. Sometimes all three. When he was around, men's hands would dip into pants pockets or shirts where, I knew, most of them kept rosaries, saints' medals, or scapulars. Women would gently clasp tiny gold or silver crucifixes hanging around their necks.

One day I asked Margarito about him.

We were building a bookshelf for my room and we'd stopped at Lebanon's to buy a quart of paint, nails, and wood glue. The guy with the scar came in just as we were leaving. Everybody, including Margarito, had done the sign of the cross, hand in the pocket, scapular or crucifix thing. Except me. I didn't carry a rosary or wear a cross, medal, or scapular.

I tossed the sack of nails and glue onto the truck seat next to the can of paint and slid in behind the wheel. "Is that guy a witch or something?" I pulled the truck door shut behind me. Margarito stopped, half in, half out of the cab.

He looked back over his shoulder. "Who?"

"That guy that came in the store. Just as we were leaving. With the scar on his face."

"Florian?" He slid the rest of the way onto the seat and closed the door. "Why do you say that?"

"Well, it seems like every time he shows up somewhere, everybody in the place crosses themselves or grabs a rosary or whatever. Even you."

"I do?"

"Yeah. You just did, when he came in to Lebanon's."

"Hmmmm."

I started the truck, backed onto the road, and started toward Roberto's Café for a cup of coffee before heading back to Llano Alto.

"Well? What's the deal? Is there something I should know about? How did he get that scar? Do I need to get a saint medal or something?"

He just looked at me for a minute. When he leaned forward and put a hand on the dashboard, I knew he was going to tell me.

"You know how things just seem to happen to some people?"

"Like what?"

"Things. Like, some people trip and fall a lot, or hit their hand with a hammer, or drop trees on their pickups or—how some people get a lot of broken bones."

I was pretty sure I knew what he was talking about. Barely in my mid-twenties, my list of mishaps was growing more impressive by the year. Things just kept happening. Like the time my finger got broken by a ram, or when I flew off Sosteno Griego's dirt bike and broke my collarbone, or the time Roberto Lynch's cow kicked me and broke my leg. I didn't say anything but I appreciated him not mentioning my name.

I pulled up at Roberto's and we hopped down from the truck.

Roberto was in the kitchen accompanied by his usual pot and pan rattling, trying to sound all busy, when we walked in. It was ten in the morning and we were the only ones in the place. Margarito slid into a booth and I went for the coffeepot. I walked over to the booth with two cups of steaming coffee, passed one to Margarito, and slid into a seat. He picked up right where he had left off.

"Florian is one of those people. He has a little ranch over there, by Ojitos Fríos. It seems like maybe he got a witch mad at him. Or something. Maybe he just isn't careful about what he does. ¿Quién sabe? Probably, he just can't help it. Fires follow him around, just waiting to happen."

"Fires. You mean like forest fires?"

"Not really—well, yeah, that too. One time, there was a forest fire. You know that big burned area over there by Cerro Pelón? Where all the little trees are growing?"

I nodded.

"Florian did that."

"You mean he set the fire?"

"Not exactly. He was hauling a trailer, loaded with hay, from Dos Cabezas to his ranch. One of the bales must have slipped and rubbed against a tire on the trailer. The bale got too hot and started on fire.

The fire spread to the grass in the ditch on the side of the road. Florian stopped and tried to put it out but it was already too late. Whoosh!" He waved his hand through the air between us. "Just like that. It took off. It was almost a whole week before it got put out. His trailer and all his hay burned up. He barely got his truck away in time."

"So that's why everybody crosses themselves when he comes in?"

"No, that could have happened to anybody."

"So why?"

"It was the snake." I jumped about a foot out of my seat. Lucia had walked up all quiet behind me. "That's what my mother told me. Are you going to order or just sit there and drink all my coffee?" she said, pen poised over her order pad.

I looked at Margarito. He looked back at me and shrugged.

"What snake?" I asked her.

Lucia held her ground. "What would you like to order?"

Darn it, she had me. Worse, she knew it.

I reached into my jeans pocket, pulled out a wrinkled ten, twenty-seven cents in change, some lint, pieces of alfalfa stems, my pocket knife, and two spent .22 shells. I dropped the whole mess on the table. "What can we get for this?"

She scribbled something on the order pad, picked the ten out of the pile, told me to clean up the mess that had come out of my pocket, and turned toward the kitchen. Margarito was grinning.

"Well, what did we order?" I asked Lucia's back.

"Two burger baskets with chips. And the coffee." She disappeared through the kitchen door.

"What about the snake?" I shouted.

Nothing.

I scooped my mess back into my pocket and took a sip of coffee. It was a moment before Margarito continued.

"I think it all must have started one day when Florian called Abelino Cordova. Florian said he smelled smoke and wondered if there was a fire."

"That wasn't it." It was Lucia again. She handed me four ones, refilled our cups, and slid into the booth behind me. I slid my back up against the window so I could look at her.

"My mother was from Ojitos Fríos and she told me it was the snake. That's why things happen to Florian." Margarito sat back in his seat.

"What snake?" I asked. She ignored me.

"What my mother told me was, when Florian was a little boy, he used to stay a lot with his grandmother and help her out around the farm. It seems that, one time, they were walking by the ditch, on their way to the garden, when there was a snake. His grandmother chopped it with the hoe and killed it. She told Florian to burn the thing or it would come back the next time there was a thunderstorm."

I took a sip of coffee.

"But he didn't. Instead, he just threw it and told his grandmother that he had burned it. It must have been about a week or more when his grandmother . . . What was her name, Margarito? I think she was a Lopez, no?" I looked at Margarito.

"Wasn't she Bernabe Dominguez's daughter?" he offered.

Lucia laughed. "I don't know. I'm not that old."

"I think she was Bernabe's daughter. I think her name was Procopia. She married Hilario Lopez. I'm pretty sure."

Ding. The bell on the counter rang.

"Order up!" It was Roberto. He slid two red plastic burger baskets onto the counter. Lucia started to get up.

"I'll get it." I slid from the booth. "What about the snake?"

"What snake?" asked Roberto.

"That's what I want to know." I retrieved the burger baskets and started for our booth.

"What are you guys talking about?" Roberto asked.

"Florian Cisneros," Margarito told him.

Roberto came through the kitchen door wiping his hands on a towel. "What about him?"

"And what about the snake?" I set our baskets on the table and slid back into my seat.

"Ricardo asked me about why people cross themselves when Florian is around," Margarito said.

"They do?" Roberto injected.

"And Lucia was telling us about the snake." I just wouldn't let it go.

"What snake?" Roberto looked around at each of us.

Lucia whacked the table with her hand. "That's what I was saying. If you would just be quiet."

We all looked at her. I lifted a chip, one of the big ones, from my burger basket.

"Are you finished?" Lucia asked. We guys didn't say anything. I slipped the chip into my mouth. Its crunch was loud in the sudden silence.

"Bueno. Better. It was more or less a week later when Procopia told Florian to go get some water from the ojito. It was almost night and all afternoon the clouds had been getting darker and darker and closer. You couldn't even see the mountains because of the storm up there. Florian took off running with the bucket, as fast as he could, to the ojito. All he could think of was the snake that he didn't burn. It seems like he got to the ojito and was running back to the house with the water when all of sudden, there came a flash and a crash. Florian froze in his tracks. The clouds opened up and it started to rain. Hard. Pobrecito Florian. It was like his feet all of a sudden were made of mud. He couldn't move. Every place he looked he saw a snake.

"From somewhere, he found the strength to make the sign of the cross. That's when another lightning and the thunder came.

"It wasn't too long before Procopia got worried. The lightning had been close. She went out looking for Florian and found him lying there next to the ditch. The water bucket, split in two by the lightning, was still in his hand. Procopia thought he must be dead. But no. He was still breathing. She dragged him, all wet and muddy, to the house. She put him in the bed and ran to her vecinos for help.

"When she got back with her neighbors, they found Florian sitting up in bed looking all around like he didn't know where he was. When he saw his grandmother he started crying, and told her how he didn't burn the snake, and how the lightning came, and he was surrounded by snakes, and all he could think to do was make the sign of the cross. Everybody in the room nodded, crossed themselves, and said their 'gracias a Dios.'

"Procopia and the neighbor women cleaned Florian up and put dry clothes on him. When they wiped the mud away from his face they found where the lightning had burned him, like a cattle brand, in the shape of a snake. That's how he got that scar."

"Remember the time he called everybody because he smelled smoke?" Roberto jumped into the story. "And he almost burned down his own barn?"

"That's the time I was telling Ricardo about," said Margarito. "When Florian called Abelino Cordova—"

"No, that was another time. I think. When he was smoking and the ashes from his cigarette fell in the hay."

I asked again. "What happened to the snakes?"

Margarito and Roberto were going back and forth about different times Florian had started fires.

Lucia leaned toward me. "After it stopped raining all the men went out with lanterns. Some took hoes and shovels with them to kill the snakes. They found the water bucket and . . . Roberto, we have customers."

I looked up. Two cars and a pickup had pulled into the parking lot. Six or seven people were headed for the door.

"Tell me about the . . ." Lucia and Roberto had vanished. They reappeared a moment later behind the counter. Roberto went back to rattling pots and pans and Lucia was standing there, all smiles, pen and pad ready to take orders.

After about five minutes of shaking hands, "how are yous," and "how is your grandmothers" with the newcomers, Margarito and I finished our burgers and chips. Margarito went out while I stopped to get a to-go refill of coffee. The bell over the door dinged behind me. I turned to see who had come in. Everybody in the place, Roberto and

Lucia included, nodded, waved, and hurriedly made little crosses on their lips, chests, or foreheads.

I nodded to Florian as I walked past and out the door to my truck.

We started toward Llano Alto.

"So. What happened to the snakes?" I asked Margarito.

"I don't know. I never heard about that before. Maybe the lightning killed them all. Or maybe there weren't any and Florian just imagined them."

"OK, I'll just ask Lucia the next time I see her. How many times did Florian start a fire? And what does that have to do with snakes and lightning?"

"I don't think it has anything to do with snakes and lightning. That's just how things got started going all bad for him." He was counting on his fingers.

"Well?"

"Bueno. The best I can tell . . ." He held up a finger. "The time I told you about, Cerro Pelón." He held up a second finger. "The time Roberto said. About the cigarette and the hay." Up went a third finger. "The time I was saying, when Florian called his primo, Abelino Cordova." A fourth finger. "Another time when he was hauling hay and the same thing happened. He was coming from Llano Alto and the fire started on the road to Río Pueblo. I think that's the one that burned Demecio's corrals." A fifth finger. "Then there was the time he was driving to La Plaza and his truck started on fire." A sixth finger rose from the ashes of Florian's life. "There was the fire that started in a stovepipe at his house. That's when his wife left him and took the kids to Santa Fe. Before they all burned up." A seventh finger. "There was the time he was at his primo's house—"

"Abelino's?" I interrupted.

"No, I think it was Abenicia Martínez. He went over for a matanza and all of a sudden, her hay pile caught on fire. Her husband wouldn't let Florian come over after that."

I was beginning to get the idea. We wound up the switchback to Llano Alto. I downshifted.

"There was even a rumor going around that the governor was considering declaring Florian a disaster area. But nothing ever came of it."

I pulled up to the Llano Alto Post Office and got off the truck.

"Get mine too," Margarito shouted as I slammed the truck door.

I was glad Della wasn't in the P.O. I was in a hurry to hear more about Florian and it would have been rude not to take the time to visit with her. I could see her through the window. She was in the yard out back hanging laundry. She looked up. I waved. She waved back.

I stepped behind the counter, pulled my grandmother's and Margarito's mail from their boxes, and headed out to the truck before Della had a chance to hang a pair of blue jeans.

I jumped on the truck.

"How's Della?" Margarito asked.

"Hanging her wash."

He just looked at me.

"What? She was out back. Hanging her wash." I put the truck in gear and gave it gas.

He nodded and looked at the stack of mail I'd handed him. "Wait."

I jammed on the brakes and clutch.

"This isn't my mail. It's Freddie Maestas's." He held up the fistful of rubber band- wrapped mail.

"Oh, shh—" I snatched the mail from his hand, put the gearshift in neutral, jumped off the truck, and jogged the twenty yards back to the post office.

It took me a little longer than I expected. I found Margarito's mail all right but I couldn't remember what box Freddie's had come out of. I must have pulled mail out of ten or eleven boxes and was trying to figure out which box was Freddie's so I could put his back before Della came in and charged me with a federal offense for stealing mail when I saw my truck roll past the window, backwards. Margarito was nowhere in sight.

I stuffed Freddie's mail, and all the others, into the nearest empty boxes and darted headlong for the door. I made it out to the porch just as the clunk (of the truck striking something), crack (of whatever it was the truck hit) and pwang (of broken barbed wire) happened.

The truck had come to rest on a cedar post in the fence around the yard of Della's mother's house. The post was cracked clean off from the impact and a strand of barbed wire looped out into the dust of the road. It lay there quivering like a dying snake in the afternoon sun.

I ran to the truck and looked in the window. Head and shoulders jammed under the steering wheel, butt on the seat, feet flailing. "A little help here?" Margarito said all casual.

I opened the door and dragged him out of the truck.

"Do you know how hard it is to push down a brake with your hands?"

"Uh, no. Why didn't you use your foot?"

"I didn't think, it happened too fast."

"What happened? Is anyone hurt?" It was Della.

"I'm sorry Della, I'll fix it. I was in the P.O. getting Margarito's mail and I forgot to put the brake on the truck."

"Well, at least nobody got hurt." She looked at me. I looked at the ground.

"My mother is coming home tomorrow." She just left it hanging there in the air.

"Uh, right Della. I'll get on it right away."

I did. And for the rest of the afternoon I forgot about Florian Cisneros, snakes, and Freddie Maestas's mail. I dropped Margarito off to his house. Then I went home and loaded the fence stretcher, wire pliers, post-hole digger, tamping bar, half a roll of barbed wire, fence staples, a handful of wadded-up baling wire, hammer, and a cedar post from the stack behind my grandmother's shed and went to work on the broken fence at Della's mother's.

People came and went to the post office all afternoon. Some of them twice. I couldn't figure why so many people were going to the P.O. twice in one day. Most people in Llano Alto only went once every few days or the first of every month. Everybody was all friendly and waved to me as they drove or walked past. I guess the story of how I'd driven over Della's mother's fence had gotten around. It was the most excitement in town since last summer when the state cop, firing his revolver in the air out the window, chased ninety-year-old (and deaf) Alberto Rael through the plaza, for running the stop sign way back in Río Pueblo.

Nobody ever stopped at the stop sign but for some reason the cop, who had just transferred to Río Pueblo from Santa Fe, had decided that he was going to put an end to that. It turned out he followed Alberto all the way to his house. Alberto got off his truck and hobbled to the door, listing to one side on his cane. The cop got off his car and shouted for him to stop. Alberto never heard him and started into his house. The state cop ran after the old man and got to the porch just as the door slammed shut.

It took me a couple hours to dig out the remains of the broken post and set the new one. I was just hammering the last wire staple in the new post when Freddie Maestas's shiny Chevy pickup skidded to a stop in front of the P.O. The cloud of dust lifted by his truck drifted over the plaza and floated in my direction. Freddie leapt off his truck and with a wad of mail in his hand, stormed through the P.O. door.

That's when I snapped. I must have really mixed things up when I stuffed the mail back into the boxes. I had a flash of Florian Cisneros and it hit me that the way things were going people would be crossing themselves or reaching for the nearest crucifix every time I showed up in town.

I could hear Freddie shouting something at Della. I could hear Della shouting something at Freddie. I swallowed.

The next thing I knew I was pushing through the P.O. door.

Della and Freddie were just standing there across the counter from each other, glaring. They looked at me, all silent. Della crossed her arms on her chest.

"What?" It was Freddie. His hand came down hard on a bunch of mail scattered across the counter.

"It was me." It just blurted out. It sounded like a just-branded calf bawling for its mother. I couldn't help it.

Freddie glared at me. "What the hell are you talking about? Everybody knows you broke the fence." He waved his hand in the general direction of Della's mother's house. "What do you want?"

"Huh?" I looked at Della. It was like a light went on somewhere in her head. Her eyes narrowed. She made a little sign of the cross on her forehead.

I was doomed.

"What he means is . . ." She stopped and thought about it. Freddie just stood there looking at me.

"Well, what does he mean?" He looked at Della.

Della gave me a sideways slit-eyed narrow-lipped look. I knew she'd figured it out. "Ricardo was helping me put out the mail."

I jumped in, "Because Della's mother is in the hospital." Freddie looked at me. "And the doctor called."

Freddie looked at Della. She didn't say a thing.

"I'm really sorry, Freddie." He looked back to me. "I must have put some of the mail in the wrong boxes and . . . "

Della glared at me. "And it won't happen again." She barely got it out. She was that mad.

You could see the anger drain out of Freddie. "I'm sorry Della, I didn't know. I thought Floraida was in Albuquerque. With your sister."

"She is. She's coming home tomorrow."

"It was a fender bender," I offered. "She wasn't hurt too bad."

We all just stood there for a minute.

"Well, I guess I better finish the fence." I turned and headed for the door.

"No, Ricardo. We need to talk." Della's voice was ice.

I stopped and turned around. Della handed Freddie his mail.

Freddie just shook his head and made a little cross on his forehead as he passed me on his way out the door.

Della and I stood there all silent for a minute.

I couldn't take it any longer. "Della, I'm sorry. I don't know how. Well, actually, I do know how. I got the wrong mail and . . . Is there anything I . . . ?" She held up a hand.

What it all came down to was, I wasn't allowed in the P.O. anymore, unless Della was there too. I finished fixing her mother's fence, raked her yard, filled the potholes in her driveway with dirt and gravel, washed the post office windows (under Della's supervision), and hung new clotheslines for Della and her mother.

It seems that my penance was sufficient because I never have had to suffer from Florian's curse of everybody making tiny signs of the cross, or grabbing crucifixes and scapulars.

At least not that I've ever noticed.

SHEEP AND SAINTS

WHEN I FIRST CAME TO STAY with my grandmother, I was fresh from the city and didn't know the first thing about raising and breeding sheep. I couldn't have told you the difference between a sheep and a goat. I still don't know a lot of things about sheep but now, as I write this, I'm nearly sixty and at least I've learned enough to know that I don't know much. What I have learned didn't always come easy.

As far as anyone knows, domestic sheep arrived in the Americas with the Spanish conquistadores. They brought thousands of the little coarse-wooled hardy sheep of the common people, the churro, with them on their treks across uncharted territory. Pretty much like a Piggly Wiggly grocery store on the hoof.

Sheep were destined to become as much a part of New Mexico culture as adobe, La Llorona, chile, pinto beans, and the annual cleaning of ancient acequias. For centuries, the wealth of New Mexico was measured by the numbers of her sheep and the wool they produced. To a New Mexican, just the word "sheep" evokes memories of traditions and a way of life that most people in the United States could never relate to. For the Navajo it's even more so. The Diné identify with the animals in a way that means life itself.

The days of large flocks of sheep are pretty much over in the mountains of New Mexico. Sheepherding on a large scale has been reduced to stories told by grandfathers who once worked in the sheep camps of Wyoming, Montana, Utah, or Nevada, sole protectors of and nursemaids to several thousands of the animals. It's just pretty much impossible anymore to find someone willing to live alone for months at a time, miles from town, with nobody to talk to for weeks on end but a dog and five thousand sheep, for a few bucks a day.

Still, in late spring, when the lambs are old enough to make the trek, one or two dyed-in- the-wool sheepmen and their dogs drive flocks, numbering a few hundred animals, up from the Río Grande valley, over the mountains into the Río Pueblo valley and east along the highway. Eventually, they turn off onto a narrow forest trail and vanish into the mountains for the summer.

Those people fortunate enough to witness the phenomenon, stop their trucks and just sit there, silently watching as the animals pass, hooves making a rhythmic, staccato clicking on the pavement, punctuated by an occasional "baaaa."

Most families in Llano Alto and the other mountain villages still keep a few sheep around as a reminder of the way things used to be and a source of meat. A handful of families still produce weavings, mostly for the tourist market.

Each spring, my grandmother's small flock produces a handful of cute tiny and very white pink-nosed lambs. Actually, every year with the warming weather, most of the farms in the valley are suddenly populated with the little spring-legged, curly-coated things.

Sheep have, more or less, a five-month gestation period. They usually begin breeding in late summer or early fall, as the days grow shorter. The breeding season can last as long as six months with some breeds. My grandmother's sheep were one of those breeds. If you don't want to be awake all night in subzero weather, warming up newborn lambs, then you take steps to control the breeding season so the lambs will be born in early spring. My grandmother took the precaution of fastening a homemade hobble from her ram's right front leg to his right hind leg that prevented him from mounting the ewes and breeding until she wanted him to, and we removed the hobble.

Getting the ram hobbled was a one man, one beast rodeo. I ran around the pen with the two-foot-long leather strap hanging from my back pocket, trying to corner the ram who refused to stand still and let me get hold of him. My grandmother stood outside the pen, enthusiastically waving her arms and shouting instructions in Spanish, which she knew I didn't understand. She must have forgotten in the midst of all the excitement.

I hadn't even figured out how I was going to go about getting the hobble on the ram's legs when, or if, I did manage to catch him. The wooly, horned beast outweighed me by most of a hundred pounds.

I remembered seeing Margarito catch a ram once by a hind leg. He'd walked slowly toward the animal, backing it into a corner. He then shifted direction slightly and the ram bolted toward the opening. Margarito's arm swiftly and surely shot out and grabbed a wooly hind leg. Once he was caught the ram jumped, kicked once or twice, and settled down. Margarito reached over the ram's back and under its belly, grabbed a leg, and flipped the ram onto its side. It all seemed so easy when he did it. And he's a lot smaller than me.

I tried Margarito's method half a dozen times before I gave up and dove, full onto the ram's back. I grabbed two handfuls of wool and hung on. The ram bucked, kicked, tossed his head, and ran around the corral, dragging me along with him. We made a couple trips around before he finally stopped, wheezing from the exertion.

Somehow, I had the presence of mind to reach behind me for the hobble. It was gone. I managed to lift my head and look around. The leather strap was lying, half buried in churned-up dirt and manure on the other side of the corral. I groaned. My grandmother jumped, shouted, and pointed to the hobble. I let go and slid to the ground. Sweat trickled into my eyes. My legs quivered. I spit out a mouthful of wool and dirt. The ram casually walked off to the other side of the corral and turned. Keeping an eye on me.

Finally, after several tries at tackling the beast had resulted in jamming my left thumb to my wrist, tearing the right knee out of my jeans, peeling the skin off my knee, and whacking my head on the corral logs, I got the job done. It wasn't pretty and it took most of the afternoon. I went to bed right after a hot bath. I didn't even eat supper.

It just happened that one day my grandmother decided she needed a new ram. I don't know how she arrived at this decision. It seemed to me that the year's lambs were all right and there sure didn't seem to be anything wrong with the ram she already had. He spent most of his days chasing the ewes around the corrals, licking and curling his lips, and making obscene guttural ram noises that set the ewes on edge so they ran around the pen trying to get as far away from him as possible. Maybe the ewes knew something I didn't about the old guy.

Apparently, my grandmother and Margarito had gotten together at some point and decided they would make a three-way ram swap between themselves and a fellow named Eusebio Medina who lived in Dos Ojos. My grandmother's ram would go to Margarito, Margarito's ram was going to Mr. Medina, and a ram from the Medina flock was coming to try his luck with my grandmother's girls. The common denominator in all of this was me.

All I had to do was load my grandmother's ram onto the bed of the pickup and deliver him to his flock of wooly brides at Margarito's. Then I'd load Margarito's ram on the truck, deliver him to Mr. Medina and repeat the process, finally arriving home with a ram from the Medina flock. It wasn't exactly rocket science. I borrowed a set of stock racks from Margarito's cousin that more or less fit my grandmother's seventeen-year-old rusty green Chevy pickup.

On the fateful morning I took more time than usual picking through my breakfast and tending to a number of minor chores I'd been putting off for the past six months. I kept looking to the sky, hoping for rain. Not a chance. It was one of those beautiful October days with a warm sun and a few puffy white clouds in a clear, pale blue sky that let you think maybe winter would wait until January. Not a chance of that either.

I checked the engine oil in the truck, checked the tire pressure, blew the air filter clean, tightened the radiator hoses, cleaned the battery connections, and split a week's firewood. Eventually, it got to the point where I just couldn't put it off any longer.

I wrestled my grandmother's ram onto the bed of the truck. The hobble had slowed him down enough so I was able to get my hands on him and drag him to where I managed to lift half of him onto the tailgate. Then I half-lifted, half-rolled the rest of him up into the truck bed and quickly swung the tailgate and stock racks closed. I climbed over the stock racks into the bed of the truck, cut the baling twine that secured the hobble around his legs and scrambled back over the stock racks before he realized he had regained the freedom to mash me against the side of the truck.

I got on the truck and, despite a steady throbbing pain shooting from my lower back down my right leg, drove to Margarito's. He'd put his ram, the one going to Mr. Medina, in a small log pen. A penciled note on a scrap of paper, stuck on a nail, told me he wouldn't be available for the next two or three days and would I please feed Solo Vino and the sheep while he was gone.

It was no trouble unloading my grandmother's ram. No sooner had he seen Margarito's ewes grazing by the river than he started calling out and battering the sides of the truck bed. As I started to lower the tailgate he bolted toward freedom. Two hundred fifty pounds of ram landed squarely on the tailgate and bounded away in a wooly white flash. The tailgate slammed down on my left knee. The ram ran toward the girls. They ran from him as fast as they could.

My back and right leg throbbed. My left leg had mercifully gone numb. I couldn't feel my left foot. Margarito's ram threw a jealous fit and started slamming his horned head against the logs of the pen, trying to get to the interloper. I whimpered involuntarily, sat on the tailgate to catch my breath, and massaged my knee.

Suddenly the bright idea came to me to use the ram's impulses to get him into the truck. I backed the truck as close as I could to the pen and made an opening by sliding the ends of the upper two logs onto the ground. The ram immediately charged at the opening. I jumped in front of him and grabbed hold with both arms. The saints were with me.

I went up and over, backward, into the bed of the truck, hard, with my arms wrapped around two hundred fifty pounds of wool and horny, pissed-off ram. I lost my grip. The ram somersaulted over me and kept going until he came up head first against the back of the cab. I rolled off the tailgate onto the ground.

Somehow, I had the presence of mind to push the tailgate up until it snicked shut and swung the stock racks closed across the back just as the ram realized where he was. He turned, bellowed and stamped at me. I reached up and latched the stock rack. He was at the back of the truck in one jump and slammed headfirst full into the stock racks. I pulled my hand clear just in time.

My head throbbed above my left eye and my eyelid drooped, half closed. I'd pulled something high up in my back. My right thumb felt like it might be dislocated and my left ring finger throbbed and looked sort of crooked. One of the ram's hooves must have caught in my shirt and torn it. A long red welt ran from just beneath my collarbone to my navel. I limped to the house and filled Solo's food bowl.

Now all I had to do was find Eusebio Medina's house and repeat the process. I wondered if I had enough body parts left to finish the job and get home.

As I drove away from Margarito's, the ram in the back of the truck bellowed in outrage and ran from one side of the truck bed to the other. He hammered the sides with his head, bellowing, all the way through Llano Alto and Río Pueblo. People turned and looked as we passed. I wanted to get a coke at Lebanon's store but didn't dare stop.

I'd never been to Eusebio Medina's house. When I had asked my grandmother for directions, she'd said something like, "You can find it. It's easy. Just go up the road to Dos Ojos and turn right at the pasture with the red horse. His house is just a little way past the arroyo. It's the one with all the sheep."

"But what if the red horse isn't in the pasture?" I'd asked her. It seemed reasonable.

"Oh just go, that red horse is always right there. Standing by the corner." She shook her head and poured beans into a pot of water boiling on the stove.

Dos Ojos is on the other side of Ojo Frío, about fifteen miles from Llano Alto. You wouldn't even know it was there at all if you didn't know something about the area. Margarito pointed out the turn to me one day on our way back from the dump. It seemed like the people that lived there liked their privacy. Every time the highway department put up a sign at the turn, it disappeared within a week.

I found the turn and drove off the pavement onto a rutted one-lane dirt road that wound through a pine forest. The pain in my right leg had become a dull ache and I kept shifting from one cheek to the other, trying to get comfortable. My head throbbed and I could feel a lump rising over my left eye. More bothersome was my left ring finger. It was swollen to nearly twice its size and every time I hit the steering wheel with it, I thought I'd cry out from the sharp stab of pain. It didn't seem to bend right either. At least my right hand was pretty much in working order and I was able to shift gears.

It seemed like I'd been driving for most of three miles when I came to a Y in the road that my grandmother must have forgotten to mention. The left fork of the Y climbed out of sight, up a steep rocky hill. The right fork followed a gentle slope down into a pretty, grassy, tree-studded valley. It didn't make sense to me but the road to the left seemed to be more heavily traveled. I took the left fork.

A mile later I came to a fence. I kept going and the fences started showing up more frequently. Each fenced field seemed to be more or less a hundred yards wide and vanished over a ridge to the north. The grass was tall and rippled like golden brown waves in the gentle afternoon breeze. I got the impression that snows here must get pretty deep and people probably didn't even consider leaving their homes for days at a time in the winter, if at all. The fences looked pretty old. The barbed wire was all rusty and the gray, iron-hard cedar posts leaned at picturesque angles against the pale blue sky, like one of those photographs in *New Mexico Magazine*. In some places, trees had grown up through and around the wire.

Up ahead, on the tallest mountains, early snows, most of which had melted, lingered in rocky crevices above timberline. The road turned sharply left and continued for a little way between two pastures. I topped a rise and was greeted by a handful of scattered, steeply pitched, tin rooftops. Smoke curled lazily from stovepipes. The road sloped gradually downhill into a deep arroyo then up the other side, where it made a T. I stopped with my foot on the brake to keep from rolling back into the arroyo.

On my left, a steep-roofed log barn, doing its best to defy gravity, clung to the side of the arroyo. The bottom of the arroyo was littered with old stoves and refrigerators, vintage truck bodies, piles of rusty baling wire, old tires, a Dos Ojos highway department sign perforated with bullet holes of various calibers, brush, and a few cast-off shriveled-up sheep and cow hides. There was a house directly in front of me. There was no red horse in the pasture to my right.

I just sat there, wondering if I should have taken the right fork at the Y. I considered turning around and just taking Margarito's ram back to my grandmother. Would she really be able to tell the difference? My grandmother? Guadalupe Gonzales? Oh yeah, she'd know.

I took a chance, turned right toward the mountains, and eventually crossed a branch of the arroyo. Four or five houses lined the road ahead on either side. No sheep. I drove past the houses and passed a solitary flat-roofed morada. Its lone window was boarded up. A huge, weathered wood cross out front leaned precipitously over a handful of overgrown graves marked by elaborately hand-carved crosses. Somewhere behind me the power poles and electric lines had come to an abrupt end.

The road narrowed and became little more than ruts that dropped quickly into a narrow valley and wound around a wooded ridge. The ram bellowed. I rounded the ridge and the valley opened up again. The road was flanked on both sides by fences with less than two feet to spare on either side of the truck. I wondered if I'd be able to turn around when I ran out of road or what I'd do if someone came from the other direction. My finger was screaming. I gave up trying to get comfortable.

A wisp of smoke caught my attention. I gave it gas and the truck lurched violently from side to side in the ruts. I topped another rise and saw a house on the right. The tin roof was old and rusted. Gray log corrals, unpainted board sheds, and an outhouse were clustered on a slope behind the house. Two dark-colored horses in a pasture uphill, behind the outbuildings, switched their tails and turned their heads toward the sound of my approaching truck.

Still no sheep but at one place, the bottom two wires of the fence were wrapped with white wool that had snagged on the wire barbs from generations of sheep crawling through the fence. Just ahead, the road seemed to pretty much come to an end and I made the turn into the yard next to the house. I didn't see a truck.

Multi-hued hollyhocks—my grandmother called them varas de San José—grew along the side of the house, and bright red geraniums potted in an array of two-pound coffee cans smiled from a blue-framed window. The mud plaster on the walls was well cared for and out front was a white and blue well house.

It didn't look like anyone was home. I got off the truck. I could barely stand and leaned for a moment against the truck fender. From behind the house I heard the sounds of someone splitting wood.

There's something comforting about wood-splitting sounds. The solid "schtock" as the axe strikes, the split pieces of wood clunking as they fall off the chopping block, a pause . . . and a moment or two later another schtock. Periodically, the wood splitter will toss the split pieces onto the conical woodpile. The pieces make a solid thunk as they strike the pile. Another hour of heat this winter.

I walked toward the sound, calling out, "Hello. Hello. Mr. Medina, I have your ram." I thought to myself, please don't shoot me.

I tried to tuck the pieces of my shirt into my pants, jammed my swollen finger, and flinched from the stab of pain.

As I rounded the corner of the house, I came on one of the largest woodpiles I'd ever seen. It must have been at least thirty feet in diameter at the ground and rose like a mini mountain, nearly to the height of the house. The wood splitter had his back to me and was casually tossing a few pieces of split wood onto the ginormous pile. He was average height but looked to be very strong, and solid. His shoulders and back filled out a blue plaid shirt. His thick arms ended in hands that dwarfed the double-bladed axe in his right hand. As I watched, he placed a piece of piñon on the chopping block. Shoulder, waist, and neck merged into a solid fluid effortless motion. The axe came down and struck. Schtock. Two pieces of cleanly split piñon pirouetted apart, curtsied, and gracefully fell off the chopping block to the ground. He turned toward me.

"Uh, Mr. Medina? I have your ram." I pointed in the general direction of the truck.

"Who you been fighting with?" he asked good-naturedly. "It looks like you pretty much got the worst of it."

"Uh, no, no, I wasn't fighting with anyone. I had a little trouble getting Margarito's ram on the truck. One of his feet tore my shirt, that's all."

He laughed. Eusebio Medina had a friendly face with high, arching eyebrows and a small round mouth that gave the impression of permanent surprise. His full head of hair was a solid steel-gray and black mixture.

"You were supposed to be here yesterday," he said matter-of-factly. "The sheeps are all out in the pasture."

I looked around. There wasn't a wooly face or hind end anywhere in sight. I didn't know what to say. He must have noticed my confusion. "That's all right. They'll be here in a little while. Come in the house. We'll have some coffee while we wait."

With one hand he chunked the axe into the chopping block. I followed him toward a blue and white, ornately carved door that had been mostly hidden behind the woodpile. His shoulders were so broad he had to turn partially sideways to enter the house.

The kitchen was simple and dark. The modest wood cookstove in one corner of the room radiated a gentle heat. A small sink set in a homemade cabinet beneath a window, a handmade white-painted trastero beside the sink, a simple pine board table with a very clean kerosene lamp in the center, and four gaily painted chairs made up the furnishings. There was no refrigerator or any other electric appliance. His house smelled of wood, earth, kerosene, and coffee. I sat at the table, favoring my left hand.

He pulled two cups from the trastero and poured coffee from the pot on the stove, slid a steaming green plastic cup toward me, and stood in front of the stove. I took the cup and held it against my swollen finger. It felt good.

"You didn't have any trouble finding me, did you?"

"Uh, no sir, no trouble."

"I thought maybe that's why you didn't come yesterday. Maybe you got lost."

"I must have been confused. I really did think it was today, sir. I'm sorry if it's any trouble. I can come back some other time." I started up from the chair.

He laughed. "Sit down and drink your coffee." He just stood there, looking me over. I told him, between sips of coffee, how I'd gone about loading the rams at my grandmother's and Margarito's and how I'd acquired the lump on my head and the torn shirt. I repeated for him the directions my grandmother had given me to his house. When I got to the part about the red horse he laughed again.

"That horse has been dead for fifteen years."

He stepped across the room, sat across from me at the table, and looked at my finger. It was turning a shiny purply-red-blue color. "You better get that looked at. It looks broken to me."

I didn't want to talk about my finger. "You sure have a nice place here. Do you work in town?"

"No. I don't go to town much, maybe twice a year I go to Río Pueblo. I stay here with the sheeps and make some wood carvings. Sometimes I work part time for my family, or my neighbors. I don't need very much money. Mostly, I trade things I make for the things I need. Every once in while I make a violin but it seems like not too many people play them anymore."

I tried to picture those huge hands creating something as delicate as a violin. "Really?" It blurted out before I could stop. I tried to cover up my doubt. "My friend, Margarito, he started playing a violin. His grandfather used to play one too. Mostly he plays guitar though. He's really good. I'd like to learn to play the guitar. Or something. Someday." I was babbling.

SHEEP AND SAINTS 139

He nodded gently. "I made that violin for Margarito. A long time ago. It waited on a shelf, in silence, for many years. Until he finally realized he was ready."

He dropped his hands to his knees. "Would you like to see my workshop?" I nodded eagerly and downed the last of the coffee. He rose from his chair and led the way through a doorway into another room of the house. I followed him through the door and stopped.

Before me was a veritable warehouse of wood carvings. The floor was lightly littered with little curlicue pine, cedar, and aspen wood shavings. Lifelike cedar santos and aspen angels with spread wings of all shapes and sizes stood three deep on the floor around the edges of the room, as if they'd been summoned to answer a heavenly roll call. A wood chain carved from a single aspen log, completely circling the room, hung from the vigas overhead.

Beside the door was a heavy wood workbench. All sizes and shapes of knives, chisels, rasps, files, sharpening stones, gouges, and an assortment of homemade tools whose uses I could only guess at were arranged in a loose order on top of the workbench. A couple blocks of cedar lying on the bench showed the first hints of shapes being coaxed from them.

There was a kerosene lamp with a round polished tin reflector attached to it on the far corner of the workbench and above it all, a shelf held a collection of tiny carved cages and boxes no more than three or four inches long. Each cage held a perfectly carved bird or animal. There were bears, sheep, horses, an eagle, and a diminutive elephant. A cougar glared from behind the bars of its cage. A deer with a delicate rack of antlers looked like it had just stepped from the forest. Mr. Medina chose a tiny cedar box from the shelf and handed it to me.

"For you," he said brightly.

I held out my hand and he laid the box gently on my open palm. The box lid had a little finger sized groove in it that slid the lid open.

Inside, carved from snow-white aspen, was a tiny ram. I gently lifted the ram and looked at it closely. Every detail was there, right down to the full-curl horns and malicious eyes that bore an uncanny resemblance to my grandmother's, now Margarito's, ram. I put the ram back in the box and slid the lid closed.

He stepped back smiling, arms across his massive chest. "What do you think?"

I was speechless and just stood there for a minute, grinning. I finally got out a "thank you" and stepped across the room to a shelf that held a dozen or more tree-of-life carvings. Each branch held a tiny, finely-carved bird, squirrel, rabbit, or other animal. I'd seen some like these, not nearly so intricate or perfect, for sale in Santa Fe and Taos for a hundred or more dollars.

"You know?" I said. "You could sell these for a lot of money."

He snorted. "What would I do with a lot of money? Buy a lot of things I don't need? Then I wouldn't have room for all these. My children." He waved his arm expansively around the room. "God gave me everything I need and the talent to carve wood. Do you think he would want me to sell those things I make with the skill he gave me for free?"

I faced him. The afternoon sunlight shone through the window, framing him in a golden aura. I almost dropped my little ram-in-a-box. He stepped aside and the light streamed into the room, gilding the santos and angels, glinting brightly off the delicate red, white and gold wood shavings on the floor.

He reached out and lightly touched the box in my hand. "My reward is the appreciation I see in someone's eyes when I give them one of my carvings. People have offered to pay me for my children before.

My carvings . . . I give freely to families with new children, to young people that are getting married, to old people that are sick or lonely, and to people who need to be reminded of the power and virtue of the saints, and all of God's creations."

He turned and walked over to the ranks of saints and angels, bent and gently lifted one from the floor. It was the Virgin of Guadalupe, about sixteen inches tall. "This one has been waiting a long time for your grandmother, Guadalupe." He held the statue out to me.

I stuffed the little cedar box inside my torn shirt and carefully took the statue from him. The detail was amazing. Her cloak was so finely carved that I had to touch it to be certain it was in fact wood. The stars scattered over her cloak and the rays of divine light that radiated from behind her were inlaid with finely split straw that shone golden in the afternoon light. Her hands, clasped lightly in prayer, were so delicately carved and lifelike that I half expected them to move. The Virgin looked gently down at a beaming cherub rising with outstretched arms from a bed of roses at her feet. Each petal of each rose stood out in delicate splendor. The virgin's face reminded me of someone, but I was at a loss to imagine who. He'd even inlaid into her robe an intricate design with more of the finely split and polished straw that gave the appearance of gold filigree.

Outside, a dog barked a greeting. The rapid clattering of hooves on the road, an excited "baaaaa" and the frantic clanking of a sheep bell sounded as his flock ran past the house toward the corrals. A long-eared goat stopped, looked briefly in the window, bleated, and then bounced away. The ram in the truck bellowed and started hitting his head against the stock racks.

I suddenly realized that I had forgotten all about the aches and pains I had accumulated earlier.

"We'd better go," he advised. "It's getting late."

I nodded. Pain rushed back into my consciousness . . . and my finger, my head, my back and my leg.

He walked out toward the corrals and I drove the truck, staying well back until the sheep had settled down and turned their attention to the hay that he tossed from a second-story loft in one of the sheds. I wrapped my gift ram and the Virgin in a blanket I kept under the seat for emergencies and laid them on the floor of the truck. They'd be safer down there than flying off the seat if I had to hit the brakes hard.

He pointed to a gate in the sheep pens. I backed the truck up to it and got off. It came to me all of a sudden that I hadn't seen a truck when I drove up.

While he was busy in the corrals, I peeked into a large shed. I suspected that the well- maintained wagon with truck tires mounted for wheels was his transportation. Further back in the shed was a collection of horse-drawn farm equipment—mower, baler, rake, and planter. A set of well-oiled harnesses and a high-backed saddle hung neatly on the wall. Most people left their old farm equipment to rust away in fields or had long ago sold it to antique dealers in Santa Fe and Albuquerque. I didn't doubt for a minute that the equipment in the barn was still used regularly.

I turned and started toward the corral to give him a hand. Before I got to the back of the truck, he was swinging the stock racks closed.

He laughed as I stepped around the truck. "Good timing. We're all done here." His ram bellowed once, turned and stepped to the front of the bed where he started munching on a handful of grain and a small pile of hay.

Before I left, Mr. Medina splinted my finger in a soft cradle of aspen and wool. He suggested again that I should get it seen by a doctor and invited me to come back and visit him.

I drove back through town, crossed the arroyo with the gravity-defying barn and bullet-riddled highway sign, bounced slowly past barbed wire tacked to old leaning cedar posts, down the rocky hill to the Y, out onto the pavement, and turned toward home.

A truck loaded to the top of the cab with firewood passed us. Its rear bumper nearly dragged the pavement and the tires ballooned out at the sides from the weight of the load. An expensive-looking car with a long-haired blond woman in the passenger seat passed. She turned and pointed excitedly out the window at the curiosity of a ram catching a ride in the back of a truck.

There was quite a bit of traffic on the road as I passed through Río Pueblo, people returning home from their jobs in Española, Taos, La Plaza, or Los Alamos. A few schoolkids were cruising town before going home to dinner. Last-minute grocery shoppers hurried from Lebanon's or Lynch's stores and half a dozen trucks were lined up at Ben's Package Liquors. A pickup loaded with bales of timothy hay passed, going the other way, toward Río Blanco. Sierra Rota glowed pink and gold in the late afternoon sunlight.

I turned the ram loose in the corrals and delivered my ram-in-a-box and the statue of the Virgin to my grandmother. She had been beyond happy with the statue and promptly placed it on the little carved pine chest, which doubled as a family altar, in my room. I drove to La Plaza where I spent most of the evening sitting in the hospital emergency room.

Yes, my finger was broken. The way it looked in the X-rays, there was a raggedy extra joint in the middle. The doctor gave it a sharp tug that made my eyes water and put it back together. He said it would take about six to eight weeks before I'd be able to start using it again. To save me some money he put the splint back on that Mr. Medina had made and wrapped it tight with tape.

I don't think the doctor believed me when I told him I really wasn't too sure how it had happened, breaking my finger. I explained that it had to have been when I was loading one ram or another onto the back of a pickup or maybe when the tailgate whacked me on the knee or maybe it had happened while I was unloading the rams because my grandmother had decided to trade rams with our friend Margarito who was trading his ram for one from Eusebio Medina, except we got Mr. Medina's and . . .

A nurse poked her head around the door jamb and called to the doc. After a hurried and excited conversation with the nurse, he told me he had to go. A carload of people injured in a wreck had just arrived. He apologized for not having time for the rest of my story but agreed to accept two loads of split firewood for his bill. I'd still have to pay the hospital for the X-rays, emergency room visit, and a half dozen pain pills that I was supposed to take as needed.

My grandmother was asleep when I got home. She'd seen a lot of broken bones in her time and hadn't been too worried about me. In my room, a fresh votive candle burned before Mr. Medina's, now my grandmother's, Virgin. Apparently, she had put the candle there while I was at the ER. The tiny flame flickered softly. Its light glittered warmly off the golden straw inlay of the Virgin's cloak.

It wasn't until I'd eaten two bowls of beans, a tortilla, washed down a pain pill, put another piece of piñon in the stove, kicked off my boots, set my little ram-in-a-box on the table next to my bed, and lay back in the dark on top of the blankets that I remembered something that had been in the back of my mind ever since Mr. Medina's.

I rolled out of bed and turned on the bright overhead light, which I rarely used, walked over to the statue of the Virgin, and bent down to get a better look at her face. I was right, she did look familiar. I looked up at the pictures of my family on the wall. There it was, in the photo taken when I was ten years old, during my family's only visit to New Mexico. My grandmother stood in the midst of her family. Her face was turned slightly to the right. She was smiling gently, looking down, at me.

Eusebio Medina had carved the face of his Virgin in a perfect likeness of my grandmother.

SOLO VINO

THERE CAME A SPRING when Solo Vino got all restless. Margarito had no idea what it was about. I sure didn't know what it was about. It wasn't so much the restlessness that we didn't understand, it was the suddenness of it.

Up until then, Solo had seemed content to just lie around, protecting Margarito's sheep and house, rolling in the mud, collecting burrs in his coat, and treating me to "oh, it's just you again" looks accompanied by a prolonged bored sigh.

"I'm worried about Solo," Margarito confided to me one morning.

"Pass me the nails," I replied.

We were tacking twelve-foot-long sheets of galvanized corrugated tin on the roof of Margarito's sheep barn. He was a couple rungs up on a ladder. I was semi-spread-eagled ten feet above the ground at the high end of the roof pitch. The boards beneath me were a little soft and I was afraid to put all of my weight in one place.

Margarito climbed to the top rung and slid the coffee can, half-full of recycled roofing nails, toward me. They got as far as my left foot. I rolled onto my side, hooked the toe of my boot around the can and slowly slid it up to where I could reach it. I shifted my weight so I could get my hand on the can. The tin made a popping sound. The roof sagged beneath me.

"You know. You really should be the one up here, you're lighter than me," I observed.

"I just don't understand it. What's going on with Solo?"

I ignored him and pulled a clump of rusty bent nails from the can. I spread them out on the tin so I could look through them and find a few that wouldn't require too much rehabilitation to be useful. Not much luck. Most of them were missing that little rubber washer thing that was supposed to prevent leaks around the nail hole. All of them were bent to one degree or another in various angles that might have been more interesting on the ground or if I didn't need to use them.

"You could have gotten some new nails when you bought the tin. They're only what, twenty-five cents a pound?"

"He hasn't been home for three days."

I gave up and tipped the can onto its side so I could fish around in it looking for the little rubber washer things and some relatively straight nails. I found a couple of each, more or less straightened the curves in the nails with my pliers and slipped the rubber things up under the nail heads.

I'd learned a long time ago, at the expense of two fingernails, not to hold onto roofing nails while hammering them into tin. I hold the nails under the head with pliers. That way you can get a really serious whack on them, drive them through the tin, and save your fingers.

Splang! I started one of the nails. The sound of it echoed off the sides of the llano.

"He hasn't even come home to eat. And those magpies are eating all his food."

I looked over to the house at Solo's food bowl under the porch. There must have been a dozen of the black-blue-and white birds squabbling, squawking, and stealing food from Solo's bowl.

It suddenly dawned on me that there might be a way to get some decent nails, or at least buy some time to straighten out the ones in the can and cut little pieces of old inner-tube to substitute for the rubber seals.

"Why don't we go look for him?" I suggested. "I'll put one more nail in this piece to hold it until we get back."

By the time I'd finished driving the nail, Margarito had gathered up the tools and set a couple good-sized rocks on the stack of tin. Just in case a wind came up.

I scooped the loose nails into the coffee can and slid down-slope to where the ladder had been the last time I looked. It was about a seven-foot drop to the ground. It wouldn't have been a problem except I had just spent most of the winter recovering from a broken leg (that's another story) and hadn't quite gotten to where I trusted a landing on it.

Margarito just stood there, looking up at me. "What's the problem?"

"The ladder?" I replied. I could forgive him. He was worried about Solo. In fact, I didn't think I'd ever seen my friend this preoccupied.

Ten minutes later we were slowly driving up the road toward the mountains. We'd both agreed that we didn't have the faintest idea where to begin looking. We figured it would be best to start close to home and work our way out from there.

Nothing.

We stopped and asked a few people who were out cleaning up around their yards. No one had seen a big shaggy gray dog with a long beard, bushy eyebrows, and yellow eyes.

We drove back down the road, through the plaza, all the way to the other end of the llano. Nothing. Not even a buzzard.

It was time for lunch so we drove in silence to Roberto's Café in Río Pueblo. We didn't see anyone along the road between Llano Alto and Río Pueblo, and no sign of Solo. Roberto hadn't seen Solo. His wife, Lucia, hadn't seen Solo. None of the dozen or so people that showed up at the café for lunch had seen Solo.

We ate a little more quickly than usual and slowly drove toward town, this time on the back road, along the river.

We stopped at Lebanon's store. No luck.

We stopped at every business in town. Nope.

We stopped at Lynch's store. I dug a pound of roofing nails out of a metal bin in the back while Margarito spoke to some people outside. Roberto charged me thirty cents, plus tax. I teased him about ripping me off. He hadn't seen Solo.

No one had seen a big gray shaggy dog.

The situation was getting desperate. Neither of us said it but we both knew stray dogs were fair game to anyone in the valley with a rifle. Which was almost everybody. You really couldn't blame them. People had lost too many sheep and calves to packs of wandering dogs.

What made it really bad was Margarito was convinced that the spirit of his grandfather Salodonio inhabited the dog's body. Over the years Margarito and Solo had developed a different sort of relationship than most people and their dogs.

I'd never seen any evidence that anybody's soul inhabited the dog but he did give me the creeps sometimes. It was the way he seemed to understand whatever it was Margarito and I would be talking about, the look of comprehension in his eyes, and the way he had just shown up the day after Thanksgiving, let himself into the house and gone to sleep on the floor in front of Bertha, Margarito's wood cookstove.

There was one time, though, when I had walked up onto the porch of Margarito's house. My friend was playing a tune on his violin and I'd swear that I heard someone half humming, half singing along. The music and the singing stopped as soon as I stepped through the open kitchen door. I'd found Margarito, violin in hand, and Solo, sitting beside each other in the kitchen.

Evidence? Probably not. But it left me with the distinct taste of possibility.

"I just don't know what could have happened to him," Margarito mused.

"Maybe he really is your grandfather and he just took off again. Like before, when you were a kid." It came out seeming a little flippant but I was more than half serious. It sort of surprised me.

Margarito kept looking out the window. "I've been afraid of something like that. Solo hasn't been quite the same for some time now. Like something, or someone, was missing."

"You mean like the grandfather part is gone?" I know . . . I know how it sounded. Almost like I had come to believe that Solo might be Salodonio.

Margarito turned from the window for the first time that afternoon and looked at me.

I was surprised. I would have expected sadness, distress, maybe even tears, but his eyes shone. Like he'd just witnessed some sort of revelation.

"Maybe we should go home and finish up the roof," he suggested, matter-of-factly.

"But?" For about the ten thousandth time since I'd met Margarito I couldn't think of anything more to say.

He raised his hand. "He'll be all right." He spoke with a conviction that I didn't feel. "He never really was my dog."

"What?"

"Think about it. He showed up on my kitchen floor at a time when I needed something in my life to believe in. For six years he gave me the gift of his company, his humor, the gift of my grandfather Salodonio. And I never would have started to play the violin if it hadn't been for Solo."

"Uhh—" Ten thousand and one times. But who's counting?

"Maybe somebody else needs him now." He turned and looked back out the window.

We drove on back to his house and finished the roof that afternoon. Neither of us had much to say and things went along a lot faster with the new nails I'd bought at Lynch's.

I got busy over the next few days working around my grandmother's place patching up her fences and the sheep pens. I didn't see Margarito during that time.

It was late at night, about a week later, when I got a phone call. My grandmother had been asleep at least two hours and I was in bed reading.

It was Margarito.

"He's home. Solo's home." The excitement in my friend's voice was infectious.

"Is he all right?" I asked.

"Yeah, yeah. He just showed up and flopped down on the porch, like nothing happened. He seems pretty tired but he's not hurt or anything. I let him in the kitchen. Oh. And he's wearing a pink bandana around his neck."

"Huh?"

"Yeah, a pink bandana. I guess I was right about somebody else needing him."

Click.

He'd already hung up.

TÍA CARMELA

Tía Carmela was a living, breathing, walking, talking, natural-remedy medical journal. She was always on the lookout for plants that could be dried, ground, boiled, tinctured, powdered, or otherwise incorporated into a remedio. She was a well-respected curandera and her home was frequented by ailing people from all over the mountains.

Was she a bruja? I don't know. I really didn't care. Some people thought so. She never seemed to get sick and her husband Palemon's sexual exploits were legendary. According to local rumor, no man's wife or daughter was safe from his advances. If a young girl became pregnant out of wedlock it was always said that Palemon had been the one to plant the seed. Palemon of course never admitted to any of the rumors. But he never denied them either.

No one really seemed to take the rumors seriously. Palemon was almost ninety winters old and as far as I knew no irate father, husband, or boyfriend was looking for his blood. I always had the impression that he more or less enjoyed the mystique of his reputation.

It sure didn't make sense to me that Carmela would cast a spell to imbue her husband with the ability and potency to tomcat around with other women, whatever their age or marital status. On the other hand, she might have had her own reasons to get him, on occasion, out of the house. Maybe I just didn't understand this bruja thing.

What was true was that Carmela could be found at all hours, day or night, gathering herbs where they grew along roadways, streams, and acequias. This only added fuel to the rumor that she was a witch. The way she explained it to me, certain plants needed to be collected at different times of the day for their full potency. Some should be picked with the morning dew on them. Others should be picked only under the full moon. Some under a waning or waxing crescent moon. Still others in the heat of the day, before a rain, or just after a rain . . .

Frequently she could be found quite a distance from home, trudging along the side of the road in her faded blue, ankle-length denim skirt, white apron, stockings rolled down around her ankles to the tops of her tennis shoes and a basket overflowing with various plants hanging from one arm, thumb out, trying to catch a ride.

Nothing deterred Carmela from her quest. She had even been known to call the sheriff's department to ask them for a handful, or two, of marijuana after a drug raid. She wasn't the first viejita to add some of the herb to a bottle of rubbing alcohol for an arthritis liniment.

Despite her unofficial bruja status, most people in the valley, the older ones anyway, constantly sought her out for advice or remedios for one ailment or another. An entire room at the rear of her and Palemon's tiny house was devoted to the preparation and storage of an untold number of remedies that she dispensed freely to the needy. The odors in the room alone should have cured most ailments.

I didn't believe any of the rumors. To me Carmela was a curandera, an herbalist, a person who understood the healing powers of certain herbs and plants, the keeper of an ancient lore. More importantly, she shared her knowledge. It probably didn't hurt her reputation that her neighbors believed she was more, or that other worldly powers were her special aids. Nobody, especially Carmela, would deny the healing power of belief.

From her I learned that pague was used to cure colic or stomach aches, pasote for menstrual cramps and constipation, inmortal would ease labor pains and headaches, and osha was good for everything from upset stomachs to headaches, all kinds of aches and pains and a piece carried in your pocket was considered to be a snake repellent. Cota tea aided poor circulation and poleo could be used to relieve coughs, arthritis, and rheumatism. All of these she taught me, and much more. The litany was endless and somewhere, I still have a notebook full of remedios that she dictated to me.

Margarito told me how, when she was younger, Carmela had set broken bones and made casts out of boiled cottonwood bark. As much as I teased her about her "weeds" I gradually grew more and more intrigued. I even accompanied her on a handful of moonlight forays. I never tired of her company but she could also be a pain in the como se llama.

Somehow, mostly by default, I had been unofficially designated by Margarito and Carmela's relatives to periodically drive her to La Plaza on shopping trips, while they were "busy" with one thing or another.

She could be nerve-wracking to have along for a ride. Her watery eyes were always on the prowl for one herb or another, even while she animatedly narrated the shortcomings of one or another neighbor, or related uses of various herbs, the current astrological signs, or made weather predictions.

I was amazed how someone who could barely see over the dashboard and was unable to read the print of most large-print books could pick out a plant she needed for one of her remedies as we sped past at fifty miles an hour.

She would suddenly point and shout without warning, "There. Pull over. Now."

The first time this happened I was taking my grandmother and Carmela to La Plaza to buy groceries. Palemon stayed home as usual.

"Too many crazy drivers and turistas," he explained.

As soon as I started the truck and turned onto the road, Carmela confided to my grandmother and me that she knew Palemon wanted to stay home because he was having an affair with Eutavio Trujillo's sixteen-year-old daughter. My grandmother pinched my right thigh in response to the revelation. A signal to keep my mouth shut.

It was a pleasant May morning and as we wound over the pass to La Plaza, Carmela breathlessly described the misadventures of someone whose name escapes me. My attention was on the too-close-edge of the road that dropped into a two-hundred-foot-below-us chasm, when Carmela suddenly spat out, "Stop, stop right here. Now!"

I lurched and turned toward her, sure that something was wrong. The truck swerved onto the two-foot-wide strip of loose gravel that led into the abyss. I jerked it back onto the road. My grandmother exhaled loudly, her grip on my right knee threatened to cut off my circulation.

Around the next curve I found a pullover and slid to a stop. Gravel and dust flew up around us. I jumped out of the truck, ran around to Carmela and opened the door.

"Tía, are you alright? What's the matter?" I asked, all concerned.

She angrily explained that I had driven past some plant or other that she needed for her remedios and that I needed to go back, "right now."

"Damn it, Tía, we nearly had a wreck. I'm not going to stop there, there's no place to pull over. Someone will hit us." My concern had changed to frustration.

Carmela insisted that we go back. "Who's going to hit us? There aren't even any other cars on the road."

I slammed the door, stormed back behind the steering wheel, and spun the truck tires as I pulled onto the road. We continued the drive to La Plaza in silence, Carmela looking pointedly out the window. My grandmother was unusually quiet.

Carmela's anger hadn't defused even after a very silent lunch and an hour and a half of shopping. I loaded the last sacks in the bed of the truck and slid onto the seat. No Carmela. I followed my grandmother's gaze. Carmela was standing outside the open passenger-side door, hands on her hips. She refused to get on the truck.

"Tell him to take my things to the house," She told my grandmother. "I'm going to walk home so I can pick my remedios."

"Tia," I pleaded. "It's thirty miles, you can't walk all that way."

"Better than riding with someone who doesn't know how to drive," she shot back.

She slammed the door and started off. Her tiny shuffling steps propelled her across the parking lot surprisingly fast.

My grandmother grinned and shook her head. "Go get her. And be nice, she's old."

I jumped from the truck and ran after her, heading her off just as she was about to leave the parking lot. She refused to come back to the truck.

I threatened to bodily carry her. She countered that she would scream I was kidnapping her. Several people in the parking had stopped already and were looking at us suspiciously. I finally gave in and agreed to stop and let her pick her plants.

I led her by the arm back to the truck and made sure her door was closed securely.

We had barely turned onto the road toward Llano Alto before she launched into a nonstop narrative of the misadventures of someone whose name escapes me.

TWO ONESIMOS

Following his mysterious absence and even more mysterious return a week or so later, Solo Vino seemed to settle into his familiar pre-disappearance routine.

He ate eggs, green chile, bacon, and toast for breakfast with Margarito, half-seriously chased magpies away from his food bowl on the porch, periodically cut loose with a hair-raising howl to urge along a passing coyote, and mostly just lay around the yard, moving from one patch of shade to another.

He even resumed his old "oh, it's just you" attitude toward me. It made me feel good to know that some things just don't change.

Margarito and I managed to shear his and my grandmother's sheep. I whacked off a piece of the tip of my left-hand middle finger with the shearing blades and couldn't practice my guitar for about two weeks. We sacked the wool in used burlap feed-sacks tied off with baling twine and stored them in a back corner of Margarito's newly-roofed sheep shed.

It must have been a couple weeks after we finished shearing, and a month after Solo disappeared, when Bennie Maestas asked us to shear his sheep. It was getting late in the year for shearing. Days were getting pretty warm. It took Bennie about a week of begging until I finally ran out of excuses. Actually, I was getting ashamed of lying to him and a little afraid he might catch me not doing something I had told him I had to do. Sheep shearing really wasn't something close to my heart but a neighbor in need . . . should probably get rid of his sheep.

All joking aside, Margarito and I did it.

Bennie had about the largest flock in the valley, more or less a hundred fifty sheep. A hundred fifty-three to be exact, not counting the lambs and a handful of goats, which we didn't shear. He was also one of the larger landowners in Llano Alto, magistrate judge, and mayordomo of the Acequia Madre del Río Pequeño. It was worth it to stay on his good side since he was the one who parceled out the irrigation water, always seemed to have some extra cash on hand to pay for work and, not to mention, might look favorably on you if you got a speeding ticket.

Sheep shearing is a labor-intensive business. I'd heard a lot of stories about shearing crews that used to travel around the country pulling trailers behind them with generator-powered electric motors connected to a shaft that ran down to a hand-held oversized broad-bladed mean-looking shearing head. Some of those guys could shear several hundred sheep a day.

With the decline of the sheep industry, most of those types of shearing crews had gone by the wayside, except in areas like Wyoming, Idaho, or Montana, maybe Nevada, where people still ran large flocks. There were a few guys around that used electric-powered shearing rigs but most of the people in Llano Alto barely had electricity in their homes let alone their barns. They sure didn't have enough money to pay a professional shearer.

Most professionals charged something like a buck per sheep, a buck and a half for a ram, and a set-up cost. Wool was bringing about eleven cents a pound. If you managed to salvage twelve pounds of clean wool per sheep you might get a dollar thirty-two for each fleece. Once you added up the cost of shearing, feeding the shearer, driving all the way to Colorado to the wool warehouse to sell your wool, and the cost of a year's hay and grain, you were in the hole.

It seemed like there was a lot of that going around.

Margarito and I used the old-timey type hand shears that look pretty much like a pair of scissors on steroids with a spring-steel handle, large wide flat blades, and sharp pointy tips. No electricity involved. The pointy tips allow the flat blades to be pushed through the wool, close to the skin of the sheep.

The whole business of sheep shearing was pretty new to me. What I lacked in style was only surpassed by my lack of enthusiasm, but it had to be done, otherwise the poor sheep would just keep getting woollier and woollier and . . . Well, I'm really not sure what would happen when they reached maximum woolliness but I had a feeling it wouldn't be too good for them. I asked Bennie and Margarito about it. They just looked at each other, looked back at me, and shrugged.

It took us most of six days to get all of Bennie's sheep shorn. Margarito sheared two to each one of mine. His looked better too. Mine always seemed to come out with a dime-sized bloody nick or two, sometimes three, lopsided and randomly spaced bumps of wool on one side or the other, and a sort of Mohawk-looking ridge along the backbone.

It's a good thing Bennie wasn't paying us for pretty.

We got a laugh out of the lambs. After we'd shear a ewe, Bennie would turn her back into the pen where the lambs were being held. First thing the momma sheep would do is call out to her lamb. The lamb wouldn't recognize his momma at first and would run around all frantic, tail wagging, and bleating until he'd finally try out her milk. That's all it would take to get them back together.

We didn't talk much while we worked. It takes a lot of concentration, so you don't cut the sheep. Or yourself.

Each night that week after work, I'd drive home, dropping off Margarito on the way, stagger out of the pickup, close up my grandmother's sheep for the night, wash up, eat dinner, and be in bed by eight. I'd try to read before going to sleep but it seemed like I'd just read the same sentence over and over until my body went numb and I'd finally drop the book on the floor, wake up, turn off the light, and then just lie there. Trying to get back to sleep.

Worse, every night I had the same dream. There I'd be, bent halfover, a sheep between my legs, shearing. The shears in my hand made a slow, rhythmic, snick—snick—snick. Somewhere in the background I could hear Margarito: snick, snick, snick, snick, snick. My hands were slippery from lanolin and sweat, my back hurt, my legs were quivering, and more sweat was running down my forehead, stinging my eyes. I'd look up and Bennie would be just standing there in the shade, leaning back against the weathered gray log barn, drinking iced tea, with lemon. Behind him stretched a line of bleating sheep that wound all the way up the valley and over the llano where they disappeared out of sight near the base of Sierra Rota.

"Only ten thousand more to go," Bennie would say, all casual. The ice cubes clinked in his glass as he took another sip.

Probably the worst part about it was always the next morning. Shearing sheep must use muscles that were never meant to be used. And they let me know about it. The pain and stiffness would mostly be worked out by the time I'd eaten a light breakfast, swallowed two aspirins, turned my grandmother's sheep out into the pasture, fed the dogs, brought in a couple armloads of firewood, checked the oil in the pickup, grabbed my brown paper lunch sack, and driven over to Margarito's to pick him up. We must have been our third day into it when I heard about Onesimo Padilla.

Margarito, me, and Bennie were sitting in the shade of Bennie's lopsided sheep barn eating our lunches. We'd started at six thirty that morning and had been working nonstop until almost two, when I finally gave in and called for the lunch break. Margarito and I ate light. Shearing requires you to be bent over at the waist for extended periods of time and a full stomach doesn't bend too good. We ate just enough to take the edge off our hunger and give us enough energy to keep on working.

Margarito and Bennie were reminiscing about the old days and people they had known. As usual, I eavesdropped, since two of the dozen or so old people I knew were doing the reminiscing. Probably because we were shearing, the talk turned to one thing or another about sheep for a while and from there it got around to Onesimo Padilla. I hadn't heard of him before but it seems like he was pretty much an older-generation legend in the valley.

"Remember Onesimo Padilla?" It was Margarito that brought it up.

"From Río Blanco? Sure, sure, you bet. I sure do remember him," Bennie replied.

Bennie had this slow, thoughtful way when he spoke that left you waiting for whatever he might say next. It felt a lot like leaning forward, hanging there in the air, waiting to fall.

"He was sure a good sheep shearer," Bennie mused. "And he always did it the old way too. With the blades." He held his hand out in front of him and mimicked shearing a sheep in the air.

It was Margarito's turn. "One time, I remember watching him, I was just a kid, and he could get his blades so sharp . . ." Margarito followed Bennie's example, shearing an imaginary sheep, except his blades just slid through the air without the snapping closed motion that I was becoming so familiar with. "He could slide those blades through the wool, just like that. And it would come off in long straight rows. He was the best."

"And he never cut the sheeps." Bennie scowled at me out of the side of his face.

I didn't say anything and stuffed the last inch of a bean and green chile burrito in my mouth.

We squatted there in the shade for a few minutes, enjoying the day, listening to flies buzzing, sheep and lambs bleating, letting our meals digest. I started feeling sleepy and leaned back against the barn.

"He was pretty old I guess, when he died." It was Bennie again. "And he was still shearing the sheeps."

My stomach groaned. "Food, more food."

"That's what killed him." Margarito observed.

All of a sudden, I wasn't feeling so sleepy.

I couldn't help myself. "What happened?" I asked. "Heart attack? Broken back?" My stomach gurgled. "Starvation?"

Bennie and Margarito just looked at each other. Then at me.

Bennie took up the story. I'd been sort of hoping it would be Margarito. Bennie took forever to say anything. "Well, you see, in the old days, those old guys, they lived with their sheeps. And they would sort of get a little loco. Nobody to talk to, except a couple hundred, maybe a thousand sheeps, sometimes more, a burro, and a dog, for months and months. All alone. Way out on the llanos or up in the mountains." He waved his hand in the general direction of west.

"Every year, after the sheeps were sheared, Onesimo would start out with his family's flocks and go from Río Blanco, over the pass and across the river. He would cross the llanos and go way up in the mountains. Nobody even seemed to know for sure where he went. It would take him all spring, letting the sheeps graze as they went, sleeping in a little tent that he would put up at night and, by the time he would get to the mountains, in the middle of the summer, the grass there would be green. He would spend the whole summer up there, just him and the sheeps. And the burro. And his dog. Then, when the leaves started to turn yellow and the nights were getting pretty cold, he would start back down from the mountains and finally come all the way back here. Well. To Río Blanco. For the winter."

"What about his wife? Didn't he have any kids that could help?" I interrupted.

"Weell, let me think—"

I waited while Bennie thought about it.

"His wife. She was one of those Gurules, I think, from Río Blanco. What was her name?"

"Estefanita," Margarito offered.

"You know," Bennie replied slowly. "I think that's right—Estefanita Gurule. Her father was that Estevan Gurule, the one that got killed up there, by the Piedra Lumbre." He waved his hand in the general direction of the fifteen-mile-long Río Pueblo canyon.

"Wow. Who killed him?" I inquired.

Margarito jumped on it. "Nobody. He and his brother Andronico were coming back one night from Dos Cabezas on their wagon. They were pretty drunk and probably passed out in the back of the wagon, just letting the horse bring them home. The way I heard it, it looked like one of the wheels of the wagon hit a rock and they tipped over at that narrow place in the canyon. Estevan got crushed when the wagon rolled over on him. Andronico somehow got the horse free from the harness and rode all the way to Río Pueblo for help but by the time anybody could get there, it was already too late for Estevan."

"¿Que lástima, no?" Bennie said slowly, shaking his head. "A real pity."

We all just sat there for a moment after that.

I was afraid they would lose the original idea of the story and we'd have to get back to shearing right way. My stomach gurgled again, digesting the meager lunch.

"So, what happened to Onesimo?" I asked.

Bennie took up the story. "It seems like, one time, when he was way up there in the mountains . . ." He slowly waved his hand in the general direction of west. Again. "Onesimo found a ewe that he must have lost the year before. Sometimes that happens. One of them maybe doesn't have a lamb when the others did and she would go off later, all by herself, to have the lamb or somehow it happens that one, sometimes even more, will wander off in a little bunch from the rest of the flock or maybe some animal like a bear scares them and they scatter all over the place.

"Whatever it was that happened, that ewe was still there the next year, when Onesimo and his sheeps got there, to his pasture in the monte. Some of those old ewes were pretty smart and they could live a long time in the mountains like that, if it didn't snow too much or a lion or a bear didn't get them."

I sat and stretched my legs out in front of me. My knees cracked and something popped in my back.

"What about the wool?" I asked. "If she hadn't been sheared?" I still had no idea what would happen to an unshorn woolled-up sheep.

"I was just getting to that part," Bennie replied.

He might have talked slow but he didn't miss a beat.

"Onesimo must have had a corral or something up there, in the mountains. Probably he had a cabin too. Most of those old guys had a little cabin and a corral in their favorite places. Sometimes you can still see them, way up in a canyon. But most of them are gone now."

"So, what happened?" I urged.

"Somehow he caught that ewe and was shearing her when the blade slipped and he stabbed himself in the leg."

Bennie lifted his left leg and pointed to the inside of his thigh. "Right here."

"He cut an artery and bled to death, right?" I interrupted. It could be the excuse I was looking for to put my sheep-shearing career on hold.

"No. I don't think so. Probably it would have been better that way, but it seems like he finished shearing that sheep and turned her loose with the other ones. You have to remember, he was way up in the monte. He had just gotten there, and this was a long time ago, maybe fifty years. Probably more. Nobody had first aid kits or things like that and Onesimo would have washed out the cut with coal oil and spread lard over it. That's the kind of thing a lot of those old timers would have done."

"Jeez." My leg hurt just thinking about it. "And?" I'd finally gotten around to the realization that listening to Bennie was better than shearing sheep.

"Well, the cut got all 'fected and Onesimo must have finally decided, maybe he better start for home with the sheeps."

"Why didn't he just leave them and go for help?" I interrupted.

"He would never leave the sheeps all alone, way up there in the mountains. They would probably die during the winter, or a bear or lion might get them, or scatter them all over the place.

"Anyway, Onesimo had already come down from the monte and was out on the llanos. He made his camp with the tent and it seems like, maybe, he just couldn't go any farther. The way I heard it there were some other sheepherders, or maybe hunters, something like that.

"Maybe they were woodcutters. I don't remember exactly. They crossed his path one day and decided to stop at his camp. I guess by then the 'fection had gotten really bad and the blood poison had set in. The poison must have gotten into Onesimo's brain or something because he came out of the tent, limping and dragging his 'fected leg behind him. He was yelling all kinds of crazy things and waving his .30-30 all around, threatening to shoot those men. It looked to them like Onesimo must have gone completely crazy. That scared them pretty good and they ran out of there as fast as they could."

"Really?" I couldn't help it. Just the thought of it gave me the creeps. Going crazy from an infected cut.

Bennie glanced at me before he went on.

"I guess one of those men knew who Onesimo was and he told somebody, who told somebody else, who told somebody else. You know how it is. Pretty soon, Onesimo's family heard about it. His brothers went and talked to one of the men Onesimo chased away. That man took them to where it happened, but by the time they got there, all they could find was the empty camp. I guess maybe his tent was there with all of his gear and some bloody rags. Onesimo and the sheeps were gone. They looked all around but they didn't find anything. Rain had washed out all the tracks.

"That man and Onesimo's brothers, they looked all over for him and the sheeps. Nothing. They couldn't understand it. It seemed like they should be able to find something, or some of the sheeps, maybe even some tracks that would tell them what happened.

"It seemed like Onesimo, all the sheeps and the dog and burro..." Bennie waved his hand in the air. "They just vanished. The men stayed there a long time, looking in all the arroyos and canyons. Finally, they started toward home. They came back the way they thought Onesimo probably would have come. Nothing. They got all the way home and never found a sheep, or even a footprint, or where Onesimo could have camped."

Bennie finally stopped for a sip of tea. I swallowed and glanced over at Margarito. He was cleaning sheep-shearing dirt from underneath one of his fingernails with his pocketknife. I'd been so intent on Bennie's story that I hadn't even seen him take the knife out.

"So, if they didn't find anything, how do you know he died?" I asked.

Bennie looked at Margarito. Margarito shrugged his shoulders and scraped beneath another fingernail.

"That's where everything gets strange."

I thought to myself that the whole thing was already pretty strange and didn't figure it could get much stranger.

"Onesimo had a grandson. His name was Onesimo, too. They named him after the old man. I think he was maybe fourteen years old when all this happened. Little Onesimo was his grandfather's favorite and the boy always helped his grandfather around the farm, and with the sheeps. He was the only person that knew where Onesimo took the sheeps for the summer pasture.

"Big Onesimo's brothers came home to Río Blanco and told everybody that it seemed like he had just vanished and they hadn't been able to find any trace of him or the sheeps or the burro. Or even the dog. That night was when little Onesimo had the dream.

"The way I heard it was, the boy dreamed he was sitting in the forest, all alone, at night. His campfire had burned down to coals and the light from the full moon was just rising over the tops of the trees. Suddenly, little Onesimo heard a voice coming from somewhere, out in the forest. The voice seemed to be all angry, like a person was arguing with someone. He wasn't scared because he recognized it right away as his grandfather's voice. He stood up, looking all around. He called out but he didn't hear anything. Just the echoes from his own shouts. Little Onesimo walked into the dark forest, keeping the light of his fire in sight. He called again and again and again. Nothing. Just more echoes.

"Pretty soon the moonlight came down through the trees and the boy recognized some rocks or maybe a cliff or something, way off across the valley. It was the place where his grandfather had built his cabin and corrals. Little Onesimo had been there before with his grandfather, when he was younger.

"The next morning little Onesimo told his father about the dream. He insisted that his grandfather was still alive. His father told him that he was just imagining things because he was worried about the old man. Then little Onesimo told his grandmother, Onesimo's wife, about the dream. I guess she probably said the same thing his father had said.

"Everybody knew that little Onesimo was his grandfather's favorite and they felt bad for him but they didn't do anything about the dream. He tried to tell them that his grandfather was alive and they had to go back to look for him in the mountains, at the sheep camp. The men reminded the boy that there had been no tracks to follow. They had looked and looked for the old man and it was getting late in the year. If they went back to the monte they might get caught in a snowstorm and all of them could maybe die. The next day, when everyone woke up, little Onesimo and his horse were gone.

"The sky was dark and the clouds hung low, threatening a storm. Little Onesimo's mother was all upset. She insisted that the men had to go look for him. Not long after they left, a storm came and erased little Onesimo's tracks. The next day the men returned home. It had been a close call in the storm and they almost got lost. There was nothing else they could do but wait.

"It seems like little Onesimo, he was pretty smart. He had listened to his grandfather and he knew how to survive outdoors. He finally made it to the monte. I don't know how he did it. Especially all alone like that. He found the camp where his grandfather had chased away the other men but he didn't stop there. He knew where he had to go.

"It was maybe a week since he left home, when he finally arrived near where his grandfather's sheep camp was. The snow was still on the ground from the storm and he made his camp for the night. He was sitting around his campfire, all wrapped up in his blankets, just like in his dream. The fire burned down to coals. The moon came up over the tops of the trees and lit up the forest but this time he didn't hear any voices, just an owl, in a big spruce tree. Little Onesimo knew he was too late. He laid down beneath his blankets and cried, until he finally fell asleep.

"Sometime during the night, he heard a noise that woke him up. He sat up listening. Hoping he had been wrong about his grandfather. It was a dog, barking. He made sure of the direction the barking was coming from, laid down and went back to sleep.

"Little Onesimo woke up before the sun had even reached the tops of the tallest trees and started off to where he had heard the barking coming from during the night. It wasn't long before he saw the cliffs rising up, behind where his grandfather's sheep camp was. He remembered how the place had felt like home when he was little, with his grandfather."

A big crow flew overhead. Its wings made a whooshing sound and we all looked up. I was surprised to see that the sun had moved two thirds of the way west. The crow cawed and settled noisily on the top branch of a cedar tree about a hundred feet from where we sat, turned its head, and looked at us. Its feathers were so dark they shone and reflected the sunlight in an impossible silver blue-black.

Bennie reached for his tea glass. The ice cubes had melted and diluted the last bit of tea. He downed the remnants in one swallow and set the glass back on the ground beside him.

Margarito stood up and slipped his knife back into a pocket. "We better get back to work if we're ever going to finish this."

"What? Wait. What happened to Onesimo? And little Onesimo?" My muscles had gotten all stiff from just sitting there. I wanted to know what had happened.

"Well. I can't pay you if you don't work," Bennie said matter-of-factly.

"I don't care. What happened?"

Bennie and Margarito looked at each other. Bennie looked down to the ground between his feet.

"OK, look, I'll work the rest of this afternoon for free." I blurted. "Just tell me what happened."

Bennie looked at Margarito. Margarito shrugged and slid down to the ground, his back against the barn.

Bennie looked over at me. "For free? You'll shear the rest of the afternoon for free?" He looked over his shoulder at the sun. "That's only one or two more sheeps. Seems like a pretty good deal for you. What about me?"

"OK, and tomorrow morning too. What happened?"

Bennie smiled. He had me, darn it. What the heck. I would have finished shearing all the sheep, alone, just to find out what had happened to the two Onesimos but I wasn't going to tell him that.

He probably already knew it anyway.

"Well, the way I heard it . . ."

Bennie always seemed to start that way.

"Little Onesimo finally rode up to the vega around his grandfather's camp. At the bottom of the cliffs. His heart almost left him. He couldn't believe his eyes. There were the sheeps grazing on the grass poking through the snow out in front of the little cabin. His grandfather's dog stood up from where he was lying in the door of the cabin and limped toward little Onesimo, barking and growling. The poor thing could barely stand or walk. He was half starved, with his bones all sticking out. It seemed like that dog would have died right there. Doing whatever he could to protect the sheeps and that cabin.

"Little Onesimo called out. He was sure his grandfather had to be around somewhere. No one answered. Then he got down from the horse and took some food from the saddlebags. He tossed the food to the dog and walked cautiously to the cabin door. He was pretty scared about what he might find in there, but he had come too far not to go in and see what he would see.

"It took a little while for his eyes to get used to the dark. He looked all around. There, in a corner at the back of the cabin was his grandfather. The old man was just sitting, with his back against the wall, covered with blankets, facing the door. Like he was waiting for someone. His rifle was lying across his legs under his hands and it looked like he must have been asleep, with his head down on his chest. But little Onesimo knew. His grandfather was dead. Suddenly, the inside of the cabin smelled like rot and death.

"Little Onesimo went over and lifted the old man's hands from the rifle. It was still loaded. He laid his grandfather over onto the floor, covered him with the blankets, and said a prayer for the old man who had meant so much to him.

"That afternoon, little Onesimo shot and butched a deer. He started a fire and cooked some of the meat for himself and gave some of it to the dog. The rest of it he wrapped up in a piece of blanket so it wouldn't get all dirty. The two of them, him and the dog, put the sheeps in the corral.

"That night it snowed again. It was one of those quiet snows, the kind where you can hear the snowflakes falling through the air. All that night little Onesimo and the dog sat together in the door of the cabin, keeping watch over the body of the old man and the sheeps.

"In the morning, little Onesimo wrapped his grandfather's body in the blankets and made a litter so the horse could pull the corpse. He tied the rest of the meat to the saddle and him, the dog, and the sheeps started for home. I don't know if anybody ever found the burro."

Bennie thought about that for a minute before he said, "Probably a lion got it.

"It was almost two weeks later when little Onesimo's family found them. He and that dog had come all the way from the monte, as fast as they could, with the sheep and his grandfather's body. They were just about to cross the river and start the last climb over the pass to Río Blanco, when one of his uncles saw him. It seems that the family hadn't given up hope and they all took their turns going out to search every couple of days, just in case."

ANTS IN A JAR

I'D CHUNKED THE POSTHOLE DIGGER and twenty-pound digging-tamping-prying bar into the ground more times than I cared to, or probably could, count. The muscles in my neck and shoulders burned. I couldn't straighten my fingers. They had become permanently curved into posthole-digger-handle-sized claws. My arms felt like something dead hanging from . . . whatever it is dead things hang from.

Margarito and I had landed a job putting up a fence for Juan de Dios Sanchez. Juan had agreed to pay each of us a dollar an hour and lunch. He had strung out a long length of rope, staked to the ground at each end, to keep us going in a straight line and placed a small rock every twelve feet, next to the rope. Each rock was where he wanted us to set an eight-foot cedar post, two feet deep in the ground. All we had to do was dig the holes, set the posts in the holes and refill the holes around each post with tamped dirt.

We'd been working nonstop since sunup. Good thing it was only May. The ground was still soft from winter snows, the days weren't too hot, and a light breeze kept us cool as we worked.

We were finally taking a lunch break.

Margarito and I were sitting in the shade under a tree munching away on bean and green chile burritos made by Margarito, corn chips, and cream-filled chocolate cookies washed down with lemonade. By the time we'd gotten around to eating, the lemonade was pretty warm. It didn't mix too good with the chocolate and cream cookies.

"I thought part of our pay was we were supposed to get lunch," I said.

I knew from past experiences that Juan's wife was a heck of a cook and always put enough red chile, sliced beef, papitas, tortillas, and coffee on the table for a crew of five. Of course, it took me at least an hour after one of her lunches to get back up to working speed.

"Juan had to take his wife to the doctor in Taos. I told you that. Why? You don't like my burritos?"

"That's not it. You know what I mean." I dropped a quarter-size piece of tortilla about a foot from an ant hole. They were those big ones with the black fronts, red back ends, and nasty looking pinchers that got your attention when one of them bit you.

For some reason I'd gotten into the habit of sharing food with whatever anthill happened to be nearest to me. It wasn't like I'd give them a whole burrito, just a piece of torn-off tortilla, a broken corn chip, or a chunk of cookie. Things like that. Right away one of them would find the windfall and get all excited. He'd run around telling all his buddies about it and pretty soon he'd be joined by a couple more and then a few more.

After a little while the whole piece of whatever I dropped would be covered with ants and start moving around, animated by all the activity. Like it was alive. Slow but sure, the food would be pulled into tiny pincher-sized pieces and carried underground. Occasionally, I'd have a piece of hard candy with me that I would set close to an ant hole. Careful not to squish any of the ants. Usually within a couple days, sometimes three, the whole thing would be gone without a trace. Except for a sticky spot on the ground.

I don't know what it was that had started me on this thing of feeding ants. It seemed like I could just sit and watch them for hours. Usually, I settled for checking on them the next day, if I happened to be in the area, to see how much of my contribution remained. It was always gone. The mystery to me was whether or not the ants had gotten it or if I had set them up to be dinner for some bird or ant-eating bug that came along and swallowed up them and whatever it was I had left for them.

I guess, in a way, I felt sorry for them. Everybody seemed to take ants for granted. Or killed them. People stepped on them, poisoned them if they found them in the house, or just drove over them and their homes like they weren't even there.

I found them fascinating. Not to the point that I wanted to dissect them or dig up their holes and see what was going on inside any more than I wanted to be dissected or have my home torn up. It seemed to me like the little multi-legged creatures had a lot to do with keeping the world clean. If it wasn't for ants, the stuff we dropped would just lie around and start stinking or get stuck to our shoes and tracked into the house.

I didn't even know much about them . . . like their social structure, or which ants got to eat how much of the food I left for them. It didn't matter. It just felt like the right thing to do and I had begun to feel a kinship with them. I figured that whatever I gave them would be put to good use.

On a more philosophical level it seemed like ants might have some special and important relationship with the earth that us two-leggeds just couldn't understand. By sharing food with them I was sharing a little bit of myself with creatures that knew things I didn't know and maybe . . .? Maybe that's why philosophy and I are rare companions.

I'm almost certain that there has to be some Indian idea about how ants are messengers to mother earth or whatever spirit it is that lives beneath us. I've even seen pictographs of Kokopelli where he looks like a big flute-playing ant.

All this ant watching had kind of started me watching the weather. I noticed how on days when rain or cold was coming the ants bunched up together close to their hole. When it was raining, they stayed underground. On days when the weather was going to be sunny and dry, they were scattered all over the place. Busily searching for food.

I took a piece of corn chip and crumbled it around the hole where I'd dropped the piece of tortilla a few minutes earlier.

"Why do you do that?" Margarito asked. There wasn't any judgment in his voice. He was just curious.

I looked up at him. "Do what?" I knew darn well what he meant. If he'd been anyone else, I would have been embarrassed.

"Feed the ants."

"I don't know. It just seems . . . right."

He looked around, tore off a piece of tortilla and tossed it over to another anthill about fifteen feet away. "You know that old saying? The one about ants in a jar."

"Nope."

He took a sip of warm lemonade. His face squinched up and he shuddered slightly.

"Did you ever put a bunch of ants in a jar?" He was barely able to get it out, the way his mouth was all puckered up.

"No. Why would I do that?"

"I don't know. I guess somebody did. Just to see what would happen."

That's what I was talking about. People just seem to take ants for granted or as something to be mistreated or killed. "So? What happens when you put ants in a jar?" I asked.

"Well, one time there was this guy, Rudolfo Vigil . . ."

I should have known it. I'd walked right into this one with both eyes open.

"He was always having these really big ideas about one thing or another. He spent a lot of time, after the war, living and working in California. When he retired he came back home to Río Pueblo. He was all full of ideas about the things he thought we needed here in the valley. Some of his ideas were pretty good. He was the one who started the talk about the community water in Llano Alto, and the Senior Center in Río Pueblo."

"Those sound pretty good." I was busy watching the ants and only half paying attention. They were really getting after the piece of tortilla.

"There were some other things too that he tried to get going. He wanted all the things in Río Pueblo that he had seen in California. At least that's how it seemed to people. Rudolfo would get this idea and he would go all up and down the valley trying to get people to agree with him. He was always carrying a petition for one thing or another, trying to get people to put their John Henry on the thing.

"I remember one time he had a petition for the Forest Service to allow more cattle on the forest. Nobody signed it because they were afraid the rangers would get mad and take away all the grazing permits." He paused for a minute, thinking. I took a bite of burrito and watched the ants.

"Then there was the time he had a petition for the county to put culverts under all the roads where the ditches crossed. Nobody signed it because they were afraid the county highway people would get mad and forget to scrape the snow from the roads with the maintainer. After a while, people got tired of Rudolfo and his petitions. Whenever they saw him at Lebanon's or Lynch's stores, they suddenly remembered they had left their money at home, or forgot a dentist appointment. Things like that.

"Rudolfo started going around to peoples' houses with his petitions under his arm. Most people were too polite to just tell him no to his face. Instead, they would say something like, 'Let me think about it. Come back, maybe tomorrow.' When he went back, nobody would be home. Or they just wouldn't answer the door."

"Or maybe they just forgot." I offered, even though I knew that wasn't it. People in the valley didn't like to be pressured into doing or signing anything and it's easier to ignore somebody than to not sign a petition. I figured it was a kind of reverse politeness to ignore a person, instead of telling them no to their face. Besides that, somebody could always argue with no and there just isn't any way to argue with somebody that isn't home or who doesn't answer a knock on the door.

The pieces of crumbled-up corn chip had almost completely disappeared and the tortilla-ant ball was making its way closer to the hole. Ants were running around all ecstatic and spreading out, looking for more treats from the sky.

"So. What about ants in a jar?" I crumbled another piece of corn chip around the hole.

"Well, it seems like after a while people started talking all jealous about what Rudolfo was getting, or hoped to get, out of all these things he was trying to do. All kinds of stories started going around about how he made a lot of money from the community water project and how his relatives all got work from the Senior Center, things like that."

"Of course." I observed. "That's just how people are."

"Pretty soon, every time Rudolfo came up with an idea, people weren't too excited about it. A lot of them got pretty nasty and if it was one of Rudolfo's ideas they right away started saying all sorts of bad things about him.

"Whenever he got discouraged, he had this saying, 'ants in a jar, people are just like ants in a jar. Whenever one tries to climb out, all the others pull him back down.'"

"Huh?"

I looked down at the ants. I couldn't see it. There must have been a hundred ants working their little ant butts off to break up the piece of tortilla and carry it down the hole.

Margarito stood up and stretched. "We better get back to work."

I tossed the last half-bite of my burrito to the ants and stood. My muscles were stiff after the break and it took a few minutes to loosen up.

We worked steadily and quietly for most of the next four hours. Rudolfo Vigil's saying kept going around in my head. I'd chunk the post hole digger into the ground, *ants*; open the handles to get a hunk of dirt in the jaws of the thing, *in*; lift the post hole digger load of dirt, *a*; close the handles and dump the dirt beside the hole, *jar*.

Every once in a while, I'd hit a rock. The shock of it would run up my arms and pop something in my neck. I'd borrow the digging bar from Margarito and try my best to loosen the rock. *Ants . . .* I'd chunk the bar into the hole around the rock. *In* . . . I'd chunk the bar in the hole again. *A* . . . I'd lean on the bar. *Jar.* The rock would pop loose. Sometimes. Sometimes not.

When a rock didn't come loose, I'd have to repeat the whole process two or three times. Even then, if I couldn't pry the rock loose, I'd try to bust it up into removable pieces. If the rock was too big to pry out or bust up, I'd just slide the hole over a little bit. Once I got a hole deep enough Margarito would follow along behind me, setting the posts and tamping the dirt around them with another bar. Before I knew it, I'd reached the end of Juan's laid-out rope. Margarito was sitting on the ground, four holes back.

"I think we can finish up tomorrow," he said.

On our way to the truck, I stopped by the ant hole where I'd dropped the crumbled chips, tortilla, and piece of burrito. The food was mostly gone and the ants were all bunched up around the hole. A few industrious ones were still wandering around, hunting for random leftovers.

We didn't finish up the next day. It rained. That explained why the ants had been so eager to get the pieces of tortilla, burrito, and corn chips underground and why they had been all bunched up around the hole when we left.

I didn't know what to do with myself. It was always like that when I had a job to do but for some reason or another couldn't get it done. Worse, my grandmother was in Albuquerque for a couple days with my tía Carolina and Margarito didn't answer his phone.

I hung around the house listening to the rain on the roof and looking out the windows at the water running in the yard, and the sheep huddled in their barn.

I read part of a book about a curandera that I'd gotten from the Bookmobile.

I swept the floor in the kitchen.

Then I swept the floor in the living room.

I put a bucket under a leak around the stovepipe where it came through the roof and penciled in a note on my to-do list hanging next to the calendar to patch the leak.

I swept the front porch.

I swept the back porch.

I cleaned the ashes out of the stove and tossed them out into the rain.

I stood on the porch and watched the rain carry the ashes off, across the yard, to the Río Pequeño.

I had to sweep the floor again around the stove where I'd spilled ashes.

I looked in the refrigerator and found the leftover lemonade and a couple handfuls of chocolate cream-filled cookies that Margarito had sent home with me. I set them on the kitchen table, ran out in the yard, dumped water out of the dog bowls, and carried them onto the porch.

I filled the dog bowls with food and wiped up the mud I'd tracked into the house.

Finally, I sat down at the kitchen table, read another chapter in the book, ate all the chocolate cream-filled cookies and drank all the lemonade.

Suddenly, I wasn't feeling too good. It felt, and tasted, like I'd swallowed a softball-sized wad of tinfoil. It hurt my eyes to look at the dim rainy-day late-afternoon light coming in through the windows.

The room was spinning. I put my head down on the table. I went spinning in the opposite direction from the room. I felt sort of . . . greenish.

Somehow, I managed to make it to my bed. I flopped on my back on top of the covers and just lay there watching the vigas and latillas spinning around. I tried not to vomit.

I closed my eyes. Better . . .

"Just like ants in a jar," somebody said.

"Huh?" I opened my eyes. I was lying on grass, under a tree. I sat up slowly.

A man in a blue plaid Western-cut shirt was pacing back and forth on the grass, waving his arms emphatically. "People are like ants in a jar. Whenever one tries to climb out, the others all pull him down."

"Are you Rudolfo Vigil?" I asked the man.

He stopped pacing and looked at me, hands suspended in the air, right in the middle of an indignant wave.

"Who else would I be?" he replied a little sharply. "Where have you been? Haven't you been listening to a thing I said?" Somebody beside me laughed. I looked over to the laugher. It was that little guy who lived in the pink house on the road to Río Pueblo, across the bridge where you turn to go up the canyon. I couldn't remember his name.

More people suddenly appeared on either side of me.

I looked around. There were all kinds of people from Río Pueblo and other towns in the valley standing or sitting on the grass. They all started talking and laughing and pointing at Rudolfo. He threw up his hands, turned, and walked off all disgusted.

POOF!

I was standing in the middle of what looked like the road through Río Pueblo but it had changed. The pavement was all full of potholes and cracks with grass growing in them. Not a beat up '63 pickup or woodpile was in sight. Not a cow mooed. Not a horse flicked its tail, not a sheep bleated, not a dog barked, not a chicken clucked.

Lebanon's store was pretty much in ruins. The windows were broken out and the roof sagged. The gravel parking lot was all overgrown with weeds. I looked up the road to Lynch's store. Lynch's didn't look much better than Lebanon's. The big plate-glass front windows were all boarded up.

A thin old man in baggy jeans and a loose-fitting faded, blue plaid, Western shirt was out front, leaning against the building, taking in the afternoon sun. Suddenly I was standing in front of him. It was Rudolfo Vigil. He looked up at me, all sad. He was unshaven and the skin hung loose around his face. His eyes were sunken and feverish.

"What happened?" I asked.

"Ants in a jar," he replied bitterly. "Whenever someone tried to do something or tried to get ahead, they got all jealous and pulled them down. Together we could have stopped this from happening. Now, nobody even cares." He coughed, lifted a thin blue-veined hand and feebly waved it up and down the road. A gust of wind lifted a cloud of dust and trash. The gust became a dust devil. I shielded my eyes with an arm.

When I looked up again, Rudolfo was gone. So was Lynch's store. In its place was a big paved parking lot and a shiny new big-box department store. All kinds of sleek expensive cars and chrome-laden dent-free pickups were going in and out of the parking lot. People went in the store and came back out pushing carts overflowing with all kinds of things. I didn't recognize any of the people. I looked down the road to Lebanon's store. It was gone too. A big gas station with a dozen gas pumps and a convenience store stood where it should have been. I felt dizzy . . .

The next thing I knew, I was standing in the Llano Alto plaza. At least I think it was Llano Alto. The mountains looked right but all around me were multi-level condominiums and slick tourist shops. I walked in the general direction of what should have been the washboard dirt road to my grandmother's house.

The road was paved. Our house was gone. In its place was a shiny three-story log cabin with a balcony all around the upper floor. People I didn't recognize stood around or leaned against the railing of the balcony, drinks in their hands. A vehicle honked and brakes screeched. I jumped about a foot and a half as a big gold car slid up beside me.

The window rolled down all by itself. A ruddy-faced overweight Rudolfo Vigil in an expensive Western-cut blue plaid shirt looked at me through the open window.

"What happened here?" I asked him. "Where's . . ."

"Ants in a jar," he interrupted. "Whenever anybody had an idea, everybody else tried to pull him down. We could have stopped all this. But who wants to now?" He laughed and took a long puff on a cigar. The window rolled itself up through a cloud of blue smoke. The car rolled on past me and turned in at what should have been my grandmother's house.

I found a rock beside the road and sat down on it.

I didn't feel too good. It felt like the ball of tinfoil I'd swallowed was getting bigger. My head spun like a roulette wheel. Cars zipped past me. All I could hear was traffic on the llano road above me. No bubbling Río Pequeño. No rattling pickups, no dogs, no birds, no cows, no sheep, no bees, no sound of axes splitting wood, no breeze in the trees. I slid off the rock and leaned back against the hillside. The grass made a crinkly sound against the back of my head. The sun was warm. I closed my eyes . . .

The next thing I knew I was looking up into a shaggy, gray bushy-browed yellow-eyed face. It was Solo Vino. His huge pink tongue swiped itself across my forehead. I sat up and wiped dog slobber from my face.

I looked around. My grandmother's house was right where it should be, looking just like it should look. No condominiums blocked the view and a truck with a hole in its muffler rattled over the washboards in the road, kicking up a cloud of dust.

"Solo. Where's Margarito?" Solo looked back over his shoulder. Margarito pulled up a chair and sat down. We were sitting across from each other at the table in my grandmother's kitchen. A fire popped in the stove and spread a cheery warmth around the room. It was still raining and the daylight was almost gone. Solo lay down on the floor, between Margarito's feet.

"Wow!" I exclaimed. "I had a heck of a dream."

"I know." Margarito strummed a chord on his guitar. The sound of it vibrated through the room.

"How do you know?"

"Because Solo and I are in it with you." He smiled kindly. His eyes sparkled.

"Are?"

He didn't say anything.

"I ate all those chocolate cookies. And drank the rest of the lemonade."

He nodded. "That wasn't too smart. So. What do you think?"

I started to tell him that it had been a pretty dumb thing to do but he cut me off.

"Not about that. About ants in a jar. Our dream." He waved his arm and the walls around the room warped and faded as his hand passed. I saw the empty town of Río Pueblo with the grass growing in the road and Lebanon's and Lynch's stores all in ruins. His arm passed back the way it had come. There were the big-box store and gas station/convenience store and the three-story log cabin instead of my grandmother's house.

I felt sick.

He rested his arm on his guitar. "Sorry about that."

I thought about it for a minute. "I don't like it." It sounded sort of lame, even to me.

"You can do better than that."

I thought about it some more.

A clock ticked. Solo snored and shifted his weight. Rain tapped gently on the roof. Leaking water plopped into the bucket behind the stove.

"Does it have to be that way?"

"Which way?"

"One or the other."

He turned his head to one side and shrugged. "Everything changes."

I looked down at the floor. "Well yeah, but why does it have to be all one way or the other?"

"Ants in a jar," he said sadly.

When I looked up, Margarito and Solo were gone. I was lying in bed. The rain had stopped and moonlight streamed through the window. I just lay there for a few more minutes, waiting to see what would happen next.

The house was cold so I got up and built a fire in the stove. It was nine thirty. I'd been asleep almost five hours.

I still didn't feel too good and decided to go back to bed.

I couldn't get back to sleep. Every time I closed my eyes, I saw Rudolfo Vigil waving his arms around. "Ants in a jar," he'd say. All indignant.

Then there would be feeble Rudolfo, leaning against Lynch's store. "Ants . . . cough, cough, "in . . . cough, "a jar." He could barely wheeze it out between coughing fits.

Then a big gold car would roll up beside me and fat Rudolfo would just laugh. "Hah, hah, hah. I told you. People are like ants in a jar."

The morning sun woke me.

I called Margarito. He was ready to get back to work. So was I.

I whipped up a breakfast of coffee and fried potatoes topped off with leftover red chile and an egg. While I was wiping the plate clean with a piece of tortilla I decided to try a little experiment.

I dug an empty jar out of the storage shed and hunted up an anthill. I scooped up about a dozen ants in the jar and set it in the shady part of the porch. I felt guilty about doing it but well . . . you know how it is. I just had to see for myself. It seemed like the cold night had slowed the ants down. They just took their time wandering around their crystal prison, checking things out. I fed the dogs, dumped the bucket of water under the stovepipe leak and left to pick up Margarito.

All day long I felt guilty about putting the ants in the jar. I didn't even tell Margarito about my experiment. Juan was so happy with the work we were doing that he hired us to patch the roof on his sheep barn after we finished the fence.

That evening, when I got home, my grandmother was there. I went straight to the porch and my jar of ants. There wasn't a single ant left in the jar. I knew it. Together, they had found a way to get out of the jar.

My grandmother was all excited about her trip to Albuquerque. Over dinner she told me about the things she and Carolina had done in the city. I half listened. I was just glad she was home.

The next morning, I repeated the experiment. I scooped up a few more ants this time and put the jar in the same shady place on the porch before I left to work.

Margarito and I had to go to Río Pueblo to buy tin and nails for Juan's barn roof. On the way I told him about my experiment and how the ants had all climbed out of the jar.

"You put ants in a jar?"

"Well. Yeah."

"For an experiment?"

"Uh huh. But they all climbed out." I was feeling a little defensive about the whole thing and wasn't even going to tell him that I'd done it twice.

"Why?" he asked slowly.

"Well, I don't really know. But they all got out. Doesn't that mean something? Like, maybe, if they all worked together, they could find a way to climb out."

"It means they all got out. Did you watch them? To see how they got out?"

"How? I was working all day with you and when I got home, they were gone. All of them. They aren't supposed to do that are they?"

"No, I don't think so. But I never put ants in a jar."

When I got home that night I went straight to my ants in the jar. It was empty.

That night I fell asleep thinking about, big surprise, ants in a jar. Somehow it just didn't make sense. The ants wanted to get out of the jar because they didn't belong there in the first place. It wasn't the same with people. We belonged where we were. Didn't we? It seemed sort of like the sour grapes story to me for somebody to compare people to ants in a jar just because they didn't agree with you or because you thought they were jealous.

Maybe it was true that some people just wanted to get ahead for themselves and other people tried to pull them down. I could sort of understand how people could be that way. But what if we all worked together? What if I tried to do good things for me that would be good for my neighbor and what if my neighbor did things that were good for him and good for me?

A guitar strummed. The air shimmered and vibrated. Margarito was sitting on a log on his porch, guitar on his lap. Solo stretched out beside him.

He smiled. "Back so soon?"

"Huh? No. I'm in bed. Asleep. I think."

Solo let out a long sigh and raised an eyebrow.

"We know. Don't you think maybe you're letting this ants in a jar thing get a little far down the road?"

"Well, yeah. But there's something about it that isn't right."

"Oh?"

"I was just thinking how ants should try to get out of a jar, even if they can't. But they did. They don't belong in a jar. But people, maybe we need to work together to make our jar a better place."

"Who decides what's better?" he asked, smiling.

I woke up. The smell of bacon, chile and potatoes was overwhelming. My grandmother had breakfast ready when I shuffled into the kitchen.

It was almost eight by the time I finished eating. I had to get to work but I decided to try one more time. On my way to the truck I scooped up another jar full of ants and put it on the porch. This time I watched them for a few minutes. They ran around all agitated. When one started up the side of the jar the others all tried to do the same and the whole mess of them slid back down. I just didn't have time to watch how they were getting out but it got me to thinking again.

The problem was that it's sort of difficult for me to think and work at the same time. Ideas have a way of evaporating on me. Thoughts kept wandering in and out of my mind all day, about all sorts of things, while we worked.

I'd have an idea about people trying to get ahead for themselves and leaving everybody else behind and other people getting all jealous of them. Ants in a jar? I didn't think ants could be jealous. It was more like . . . I'd pull up another sheet of tin and lay it down, overlapping the last one. Maybe people got jealous of other people because they didn't think much of themselves and . . . I'd whack a row of nails into the sheet of tin.

Next, I'd get an idea about everybody in the valley scrambling all at once to get free of a crystal prison and out into a world that we could all see through the walls of the prison. There we were, all stumbling over each other, pulling each other down, trying to get out of someplace that we didn't know anything about. Ants in a jar? Another row of nails and pull up another sheet of tin, lay it over the last sheet. Dig in an old coffee can for more nails.

Then the idea came up about everybody deciding to get out of our little crystal world and helping each other climb up, if that's what they wanted. Ants in a jar? Not exactly. Whack, whack, whack. More nails in another sheet of tin.

What if some people didn't want to get out? Leave them behind? Whack. Whack, whack, whack.

Maybe getting out wasn't the real problem. Maybe the real problem was whether or not we could let people live how they wanted to live, even if it meant getting left behind in a jar. Or leaving the rest of us behind while they got further and further up the side of the jar. Whatever. Whack, whack, whack, whack.

But how did the ants get out of the jar on the porch? No ants in a jar.

It went on like that all day long. We finished up early and Margarito came over to our house for dinner.

I hopped out of the truck and hurried around to the back porch. The ant jar was empty. I was just standing there holding the jar when Margarito came around the corner of the house.

I held the jar out to him. "See? Gone. Every one of them."

He took the jar from me. "Did you try using a taller jar?"

My grandmother stepped through the door onto the porch, wiping her hands on her apron.

"What's happening out here?"

She looked at the jar in Margarito's hand. She looked at me.

"Ricardo. Are you the one that keeps putting ants in that jar? Every day I dump them out and the next day, there they are again. The poor things, they were all frantic. Why did you do that?"

I looked at Margarito.

Margarito looked at me.

We laughed and went in to dinner.

LA SEPOLTURA

THE WEATHER GUY ON THE RADIO had predicted a high in the mid-nineties. By eight it was already hot. Worse, it was humid. Yesterday we'd had one of those brief hope-inspiring July afternoon downpours. Sweat stung the corners of my eyes. My lips tasted salty. I tossed another shovelful of dirt . . .

I'd been asleep when Margarito called. He had a job for us. And it paid cash. He didn't say what we'd be doing but paying work was hard to find in the seventies. I jumped on it.

"Good," he said. "Pick me up at five thirty tomorrow morning. Bring your shovel. I'll bring lunch."

I said okay. He hung up. I went back to bed.

The sun was barely cresting the mountains when I drove up to his house. He threw a shovel in the truck bed, slid a duct-tape-patched cooler across the seat, hopped into the cab, and waved his hand in the general direction of a hundred-eighty-degree turn. "Vamos."

I gunned the truck. We skipped over the washboard caliche road. I shifted into third. "So where's the job?"

"At the church. We're digging a sepoltura."

"A what?"

"A grave. For Eliseo's grandson."

"A grave," I groaned. "Why didn't you say that last night?"

"You didn't ask."

He had me there.

"Why doesn't Eliseo hire a backhoe? Or have the funeral home guys dig the thing?"

"What's the matter with you?"

"It's . . . a grave."

"It's just another hole. I thought you needed money."

"Yeah, well. How much is Eliseo gonna pay us?"

"Twenty bucks. Each. And he can barely afford that after paying the funeral home." His voice dropped to a whisper. "The boy was only eight years old."

"Aw, jeez. What happened?"

The way Margarito told it, the kid's older sister was driving him to his violin lesson when they were T-boned by a two-ton truck that ran a light. The boy was killed instantly. His sister was still in the hospital, recovering. It looked like Eliseo would have to mortgage his farm to pay all the bills. I downshifted, turned in to the plaza, and pulled up in front of the church.

As New Mexico churches go, San Juan Nepomuceno was small, barely more than a chapel tucked away at the east edge of the Llano Alto plaza. Its weathered adobe walls sat patiently beneath a rusty tin roof, crowned by a leaning paint-starved cupola that had at one time served as a bell tower. In the distance behind the church rose the twelve-thousand-foot peak, Sierra Rota. The church had served the people of Llano Alto for most of three hundred years but was barely used anymore except for Mass on the feast day of its patron and an occasional wedding or funeral.

The camposanto was a patch of weedy ground beside the church, defined by ancient cedar posts and a sagging sheep-wire fence. I hadn't paid much attention to the cemetery before but it was easy to see why a backhoe was out of the question. Even if Eliseo could afford it. Most of the graves had long ago lost their carved wooden markers to the ravages of time and weather. Nobody remembered whose remains occupied what space or wanted to be the one who dug up somebody's great-aunt Ophelia or great-great-grandfather Tiburcio. Digging by hand would cause a lot less damage if we happened across a century-old casket, but still, we had to be careful where we dug, or waste a day's work. By the time we hunted around and found a place that wasn't sunk in or mounded up with rocks it was an hour past sunup. We went to work right away.

When I'm working like that, my mind has a way of wandering from one thing to another. I don't have a lot of control over it. I knew I shouldn't have been bothered by digging a grave. It was just another hole and Margarito was right. We'd dug holes before. It didn't help. I couldn't stop thinking about mortality and what I was, or wasn't, doing with my life. It wasn't something I usually spent much time on but nothing else came to mind. What really got to me was the poor kid had been only eight and here we were, digging his grave.

I tried to think about something like fishing, or how much I disliked shearing sheep, or that cute girl that worked at the hardware store in La Plaza. It wasn't any good. I kept coming back to how short life could be. With each shovelful it grew worse. I thought about my mother. How her had life had been cut off by cancer. I thought about losing Margarito, who was nearly three times my age. Or my grandmother, who'd made it even further over the hill. It seemed like they were living on borrowed time. And me? I'd used up three times as many lives as Eliseo's grandson without doing anything worthwhile. It got sort of depressing.

To make things worse there was Solo Vino. Usually, Solo spent his days lounging in the shade at home, barely rousing himself for a drink or to chase magpies from his food. He never showed the least interest in going with us when we went to work. Today he'd followed us to the cemetery, running along behind the truck. Each time I looked up to toss another shovelful of dirt from the grave there he was, lying in the shade beneath my pickup. His bushy-browed yellow eyes watched as we dug our way down. He was making me uncomfortable.

I tossed a shovelful of dirt over the side. "Why is Solo watching us like that?" I asked Margarito's back.

He leaned on his shovel and glanced at Solo. He looked back over his shoulder at me and shrugged. "Maybe he knows somebody that's buried here."

That shut me up. But it got me thinking again. This time about Margarito's grandfather, Salodonio. He had been famous, skilled, a musical phenomenon. What did it get him? He lost his beloved violin, his family . . . maybe even a part of his soul.

Nobody had seen the old guy in years or knew what happened to him. He had just disappeared. And now, Margarito believed he had been reincarnated, or whatever, as Solo Vino. I had to admit, Solo could be unusual at times, and there was the matter of him "singing" while Margarito played his guitar or violin, but I refused to think of him as anything but a dog.

I put my shovel down, jumped out of the hole, and walked over to the cooler and jug of water that we had stashed in the meager shade of a stunted lilac beside the church.

"Me too," Margarito called. I took a pull from the jug and carried it over to him. Solo's eyes followed every step I took. I guess it was because I had been thinking about it that I asked, "You still think Solo is your grandfather?"

"Uh huh," Margarito mumbled around the mouth of the jug. "I know he is." He handed the jug back. I carried it to the shade. I just couldn't see it. A man reincarnated as a dog? Oh well, what goes around . . .

Margarito was sitting on the edge of the grave, rubbing his eyes, when I returned. "I don't feel so good. I think it's the heat."

"You are pretty pale. Look. There's barely enough room for both of us to dig. Go sit in the shade for a while."

"You sure?"

I nodded and tossed his shovel a few feet away. "I'm sure."

He walked over to the patch of shade and lay down. I went back to digging. For the next couple hours, I worked at an easy steady pace.

I tried to not think of the heat or that I was digging a boy's grave or that we'd have to start over someplace else if we dug our way down to . . . I wasn't even going there. Somehow, I got around to thinking about Salodonio, again.

The whole thing kept playing on rewind in my head as I worked. I couldn't shut it off. And Solo? He just lay there watching me.

Worse, I had developed a sort of habit while hitchhiking to New Mexico. A lot of time had been spent walking along or sitting beside long lonely stretches of road with nobody to talk to but myself. Most of the time it had been entertaining and helped pass the long hours but if I didn't shut it down, at some point it could become a pain.

It was as if there was a little voice in my head, like one of those cartoons where the devil or an angel is sitting on someone's shoulder, whispering in their ear. Except this was my ear. Or head. Whatever.

Salodonio was the most famous violinista in the mountains.

"I know. Margarito told me but . . ." I heaved a shovelful of dirt over my shoulder.

At eight years old, Salodonio began playing a drum with his uncles and . . .

"I told you. I know."

One of his uncles gave him an old handmade fiddle. By the time he was twelve—

"Yeah, I know. He was all famous and bought a violin. People called the violin la Esposa.

"Why are you telling me all this? I already know it." I tossed a shovelful of dirt out of the hole.

"Margarito told me." Another shovelful onto the pile.

And . . .

"Leave me alone. I have work to do." Another shovelful.

Are you sure you know all of it?

"Well, I know what Margarito told me." And another.

And he told you the truth.

"Good. I'm glad. I never doubted it." A shovelful to the left.

Hah! What good is truth if you only choose to believe part of it?

"What the heck is that supposed to mean?" About half of that shovelful fell back into the grave.

What good is it to hear the truth if, when you hear it, you do not see? And what good does it do for you to see and still choose not to believe?

"Holy—What the h—"

Don't say it. You are on . . . Well actually, you are in, holy ground.

"—Are you talking about?" I tossed two shovelfuls this time. One to the right. One to the left.

What are you digging?

"A grave. For a boy. Now leave me alone." Two more quick shovelfuls of dirt.

Bueno. I can see that you are serious about your work. As you should be. Digging a grave is a serious thing. But a grave is not always the end. Nothing is ever the end.

"Wait. What isn't? Ever the end of what?"

Silence.

Finally.

I went back to digging in earnest but the voice had gotten me to thinking again. I never would have said it to Margarito, but it had always seemed to me that Salodonio had paid the price for caring more about fame and a violin than his wife and family. But maybe that was unfair. I never knew Salodonio. He could have loved his family and loved his music. Margarito loved his grandfather and loved music. He had loved his mother and father and still became a well-known guitarist. If I was a famous musician, would I love my grandmother less? Or my mother, my father?

That's when it hit me. The poor kid whose grave we were digging had been on his way to a violin lesson. And, he was eight years old. The same age as Salodonio when he started playing music. The hairs rose on the back of my neck. Despite the heat, I shivered.

I glanced over at Solo. He hadn't moved.

I decided right then that I was never going to take up the violin. It was too dangerous. And, if I had to get reincarnated, I sure didn't want to come back as a dog.

I looked up to the sun from between the mounds of dirt I'd lifted out of the grave. Noon. Maybe a little after. Puffy white clouds, passing lazily overhead to the east, were piling up against Sierra Rota at the head of the valley. The peak was hidden beneath a blanket of deepening gray. The grave was more or less chest deep and I was hungry. I figured another couple feet and we could call it done. I crawled out of the hole and made my way over to the lilac. Margarito was stretched out, asleep. I lightly kicked his foot. He opened his eyes.

"Time for lunch." I picked up the cooler and carried it around to the slightly more shady north side of the church. Margarito grabbed the water jug and followed me.

He slipped the lid off the cooler. "How much deeper do we have to go?"

"A couple feet, I think."

We lunched on bean and green chile burritos washed down with warm water from the jug. I was almost too hot and tired to eat.

"How long ago did your grandfather disappear?"

"Oohh, at least forty, maybe fifty years. I was pretty young. But I've never believed he just disappeared. For a long time after he left, people told stories about him. Some said they had heard a violin up one canyon or another in the mountains. Others told how they had been awakened at night by someone playing a violin outside their house. When they would open the door to see who it was, the music would stop." He looked around and waved his hand in a broad half circle.

"Right here, on the plaza, some people said they had seen him dancing and playing la Esposa in the moonlight, on the feast of San Juan."

"Do you think he's still alive?"

"No. He'd be way over a hundred. Nobody has even mentioned him for years."

"And la Esposa?"

"Nobody knows what he did with her."

"Maybe he burned her. It's what I would do."

"Maybe."

"Maybe somebody, like your grandmother, killed Salodonio."

He just looked at me all silent for a minute. "Where do you get these ideas? She was in Santa Fe when he left."

I knew it had been crazy. Maybe it was the heat.

We finished up lunch and started back to the grave. I rounded the corner of the church. There was Solo, up on the mound of dug-out dirt, digging away, throwing dirt back in the grave as fast as he could.

"What the—? Solo, get away from there." I shouted and ran towards him, waving my arms. He stopped throwing dirt, held his ground and bared his teeth. I stopped. He growled. I took a step back.

"Solo, what are you doing?" It was Margarito. "Come here." Solo jumped from the pile and went straight to the shade under the pickup.

I walked up to the edge of the grave and looked in. "Why did he do that?"

Margarito shrugged. "How bad is it?"

"About a foot. He threw in about a foot. Mira!" I pointed and stood looking into the grave. "I was almost done."

LA SEPOLTURA 207

Margarito shook his head. "You rest. I can finish up." He looked around for his shovel.

Thunder murmured in the distance. I looked up to Sierra Rota. The mountain had vanished behind an unfurling shroud of thick gray clouds that were slipping back down the valley, in our direction. I grabbed my shovel and jumped into the grave. I went at it with everything I had. Between being angry at Solo and trying to beat the coming storm I had the loose dirt cleared out in ten minutes. Thunder rumbled, louder this time, rebounding from one side of the valley to the other. I attacked the last couple feet.

Margarito came up to the edge of the grave with his shovel. "Let me..."

Clunk.

I froze. Before I even thought about it, I made a quick sign of the cross.

"What is it?" Margarito asked.

"Jesus, Mary, and Joseph what do you think it is? We're digging a hole in a cemetery."

I looked up at him. He was leaning over, hands on his knees, to get a better look. Solo stood beside him.

"Maybe it's just the end and you can slide over a little."

I backed up a few inches and drove the shovel into the ground. Something crunched and gave way. The shovel slipped out of my hands. I lost my balance and went to my knees. My right hand went down, through half-rotten wood.

"Oh crap!" I froze. "That sounded like bones. Didn't that sound like bones?" I was pretty close to losing it. Margarito whispered. "Who is it?"

"How the . . . ?" Solo let out an ear-splitting howl and leaped into the grave. I leaped out of the grave. I think. All I knew was suddenly there I was, standing next to Margarito. Solo was in the grave, digging furiously. Pieces of half-rotten wood and dirt flew into a pile behind him.

"What's he doing?" I shouted.

Margarito pointed. "What's that?"

"What?" I looked down at a cloth bundle clutched in my right hand. I must have grabbed hold of it when Solo jumped into the grave. I fought the urge to fling the thing from me and took another look. It was a stained piece of handwoven embroidered fabric. And something else. I laid the cloth on the ground, held my breath, and carefully unrolled it. Despite its age the multicolored threads of the bandana-size embroidery were still vivid. Pieces of ebony and beautifully patterned fragments of maple glinted in the sunlight. I exhaled. At least it wasn't bones. I picked up a piece and held it out to Margarito. He took it from me.

"That's part of a tuning peg." He kneeled and sorted through the fragments. "Here's another . . . and pieces of a bridge. These are pieces of a violin."

We just looked at each other.

"How did Solo know?" I was cut short by excited barking from the depths of the grave. I left Margarito sorting through the pieces and went to look.

Solo had pretty much uncovered the remnants of a foot and a half by ten-inch wooden box. He looked up at me, panting. I eased myself into the grave, knelt beside him, and brushed aside dry-rotted fragments of wood with my hand. Solo sat quietly, watching, as I excavated the contents of the box.

"Margarito, you gotta see this."

He dropped into the grave, knelt beside me and carefully rummaged around in the remains.

"It is a violin."

"It was a violin." I mumbled. I was trying to wrap my head around how Solo had known about the box.

Margarito held up most of a violin scroll and a couple pieces of wood. "This is her," he whispered. "It's la Esposa." He knelt down with the shattered pieces of wood cradled in his lap. "After all these years." A flash of blue light lit the depths of the grave. Thunder crackled and rumbled, echoing down the valley. A few heavy drops of rain spattered around us.

"How do you know it's la Esposa?"

"Here, etched in the scroll. My grandfather's name, Salodonio Valdez." He held it up so I could see.

"Holy . . . What do you want to do with her? Maybe you should take her home."

"No, I don't think so. I think we were supposed to find her. She's supposed to be here, with Eliseo's grandson. And we can't tell anybody." He pulled the embroidered cloth from a hip pocket. "See?" It was a beautifully done likeness of San Juan Nepomuceno, patron of the little church and the Penitentes, forefinger held to his lips, swearing us to secrecy. "We have to get a new box and bury her right here, deeper, so nobody will find her. And something to cover the grave, to keep it safe from the rain."

"Tin. I'll get a couple sheets left over from when I roofed the barn. There's a box with a lid in my grandmother's shed." I scrambled out of the grave and ran for the truck. "You dig!" I shouted over my shoulder.

I slid the truck to a stop beside my grandmother's house and ran to the shed. I dumped twenty years of mouse droppings, bent rusty nails, and dead moths out of the box. I dropped a hammer and nails in the box and tossed it in the pickup as I passed on my way to get the tin. I'd just slid the tin into the truck bed when my grandmother stepped out on the porch.

"Ricardo, where are you going with that tin?"

I jumped into the truck. Fat raindrops splattered on the windshield. I slammed the door behind me and shouted out the window to her as I drove past. "We need it Grandma. We found . . ." I thought suddenly of the likeness of San Juan Nepomuceno, finger to his lips. "To cover a grave." I gunned the truck and headed up the road to the church.

I backed the truck up as close as I could and hopped from the cab. Thunder rumbled overhead. A shovelful of dirt flew out onto a pile. I carried the box to the side of the grave. Another shovelful of dirt flew past, narrowly missing me. I looked into the grave. "Wow, that's deep."

Margarito and Solo looked up from the depths. "We couldn't get out. So, I just kept digging."

I passed the box, hammer, and nails down to him and dropped into the grave beside them. It only took us a minute to wrap the remains of la Esposa in the embroidery and place her in the box. Margarito nailed the lid shut and laid her to rest in the niche he had dug for her.

The three of us stood together in the grave. Our breathing sounded loud. La Esposa lay silent in her new box.

"Shouldn't we say something?" I asked.

Margarito spoke up. "Thank you . . . and please take care of Eliseo's grandson."

Lightning flashed, followed immediately by the crack and boom of thunder. Heavy raindrops spattered around us. I grabbed a shovel and backfilled la Esposa's tomb, packing the dirt with my feet. I hoisted Margarito and Solo out of the grave, passed the shovel and hammer up, and scrambled over the edge just as Margarito ran up with the tin. We hurried to get the grave covered and dirt piled around the edges of the tin. We barely made it to the truck before the rain really started to come down.

We just sat there in the pickup, Solo between us, watching the rain, its intensity rising and falling. Gregorian chant in liquid form. A blessing to crops and forest. Thunder rumbled, deep in the clouds. The beat of a pueblo drum. The earth shuddered with gratitude.

I felt like I should say something to Margarito about Salodonio, la Esposa, and how Solo had known about the box. How maybe Margarito was right about Solo and how maybe there are things in life that shouldn't need to be explained and just accepting them ought to be enough and how I was sorry I hadn't believed him. But I wouldn't let it come out. I reached for the key to start the truck.

"I told you." Margarito said softly.

I looked over at him, my hand on the ignition. I didn't say anything. I knew what he meant. Solo cocked his head and looked sideways at me, eyebrows raised. In the rearview mirror I watched the rain running off sheets of tin covering a grave. The rain became rivulets that flowed under and around the truck, into the plaza. There they joined a dozen other streams of muddy water that flowed together out of the plaza and over the edge of the llano.

"Tell Eliseo to keep his money," I said suddenly. "I don't need it that bad and . . ." I left it hanging there, not sure of what I wanted to say. Margarito and Solo just looked at me.

It came out of me in a whisper. "I don't even know the kid's name."

"Sal." Margarito said softly. "His name was Salodonio."

GLOSSARY OF TERMS AND WORD USES IN NEW MEXICO

acequia madre	mother ditch, main irrigation ditch
alabado(s)	hymns of praise to God, the Virgin Mary, or the saints, usually sung without instrumental accompaniment
baile	dance
bisabuelo(a)	great-grandfather, great-grandmother
bizcochito	anise-flavored cookie or biscuit, often with a sprinkling of sugar and/or cinnamon. The best are made with lard.
bruja	simply put, a witch
bueno	good, OK
buenos días	good day, good morning
butched	butchered
calabacita(s)	squash(es)

caliche	calcium carbonate, the remains of shells of many billions of dead sea-dwelling creatures from the time of the Great Inland Sea that covered much of New Mexico. It is quarried and used as an amazingly durable road surfacing material.
camposanto	literally a "holy field"; a cemetery
capulín	chokecherry
carne seca	dried meat, jerky
Cerro Pelón	Bald Hill; in this book, a fictitious hill
chicos	dried roasted sweet corn
coke	in daily conversation this means any brand or flavor of soft drink
como se llama	how do you call it, whatchamacallit; butt, rear end
cota	an herb; also referred to as Navajo or Indian tea
coyote	the dog-like animal; also used in New Mexico to denote a person of mixed blood, usually Spanish-American and Anglo
cuadrilla	quadrille; a dance
cuna	cradle; a dance
curandera(o)	a healer
despedida	a song of saying goodbye; as used here, to a deceased person

Dia de los Santos Reyes	Three Kings Day, January 6
Dos Cabezas	Two Heads; in this book, a fictitious town
demonio	demon
embarazada	pregnant
fiesta(s)	celebration of the feast day of the patron saint of a village or church. Often has a parade, carnival rides, booths with items to buy and plenty to eat. Attended by all the residents of a community; many persons who have left town to live elsewhere return annually for the fiestas to see family and friends.
función	function; a gathering, a celebration, often includes dancing
gracias a Dios	thanks be to God
granpo	grandpa
gringo	a non-Hispanic; an outsider; non New Mexico native
havas	large, nutritious, and flavorful bean; sometimes referred to as horse beans

los Hermanos	a group known by many names, including los Hermanos de Luz, although most commonly los Penitentes or los Hermanos. A fraternal order of laymen who focus on penance and the suffering and crucifixion of the Christ. For a long period in New Mexico's history, priests were scarce and los Hermanos performed many of the rites of the church. They also supplied a great deal of social organization in isolated communities and provided for those in need. Much has been written about them, a lot of it based in gross misunderstanding and exaggeration. The full name is la Cofradía de Nuestro Padre Jesús Nazareno.
indita	literally, Indian maiden; musical form with a Native American rhythm
inmortal	an herb; also called antelope horn, creeping milkweed
John Henry	locally used in some areas for John Hancock, signature
Kokopelli	Native American figure often depicted as a humpbacked flute player, frequently found in petroglyphs. Generally considered a fertility figure. In more recent times a symbol of the Southwest that appears on a vast number of art and tourist items.
Lady of Guadalupe	also called the Virgin of Guadalupe. Declared the patroness of the Americas by Pope John Paul II. It is said that she appeared to Juan Diego in 1531 and asked that he request the building of a chapel dedicated to her. The bishop asked for proof of her appearance. Juan Diego returned with a robe full of roses (in December) and showed them to the bishop. The now well-known portrait of her was miraculously imprinted on his robe. Although there is some disagreement as to when (even the century) she appeared and the circumstances surrounding her appearance, she has become integral to the culture of Mexico and the US Southwest.

La Plaza	The Plaza; in this book, a fictitious town
latilla(s)	small, peeled pole(s), commonly of aspen, used as roofing material to overlay vigas in ceilings; often overlaid with tar paper and several inches of earth
Llano Alto	High Plain; in this book, a fictitious village
la Malinche	character in the Matachines. Differing information has been circulated regarding her. Generally, it is accepted that she was a slave in the service of Hernán Cortés and bore his son. She was reportedly a translator between Cortés and Montezuma and is frequently disparaged for having betrayed the Aztec leader to Cortés. In the Matachines she is usually depicted by a young girl.
los Matachines	a dance, something of a folk play. There are many variations of the Matachines, including when it is performed and its form, although there are basic similarities. In general, the dance represents the clash between Spanish and Native American cultures.
matanza	slaughtering of an animal, usually a pig or lamb; community event of ancient origins in which all comers are fed, catch up on local news, and share recipes. What is billed as the "World's Largest Matanza" takes place annually in Belen, New Mexico.
mayordomo	in this instance refers to a ditch boss; can denote person(s) responsible for maintenance of a church; overseer
merced	common lands where community members would gather firewood, timber for building, hunt, and graze livestock. Much of the merced in New Mexico was not recognized by the United States and became what we now know as National Forest.

milagro	miracle; also small figures of body parts (hands, head, feet, arms, etc.) for which prayers are offered to effect a healing
mira	look!
el monarca	the monarch, Montezuma; from the folk play/dance los Matachines
monte(s)	mountain(s), sometimes used to signify a range of mountains
morada	a chapel of los Hermanos
Ojito(s) Frío(s)	Little Cold Springs; in this book, a fictitious town
Ojo Colorado	Red Spring; in this book, a fictitious town
Ojo Frío	Cold Spring; in this book, a fictitious town
osha	an herb; also known as Porter's lovage
pague	an herb; also known as fetid marigold
pajarito(s)	little bird(s)
papas fritas	fried potatoes, also papitas
pasote	an herb; also known as epazote, Mexican tea, American wormseed
los Penitentes	see los Hermanos
pobrecito(a)	poor him, poor her
poleo	an herb; also known as brook mint

primo(a)	male cousin, female cousin
¿quién sabe?	"who knows?"
remedio(s)	remedies
Río Blanco	White River; in this book, a fictitious village
Río Pequeño	Tiny River; in this book, a fictitious stream
Río Pueblo	River Town; in this book, a fictitious village
San Juan Nepomuceno	St. John of Nepomunk. It is difficult at best to find reference linking him to los Hermanos. However, it has been told to me that he is generally recognized as their patron, at least in the community where I first settled in New Mexico. I have seen art by los Hermanos which depicts him as I described, forefinger to his lips, urging silence.
San Martín Caballero	St. Martin the horseman, or gentleman. Also St. Martin of Tours. It is said that he was a Roman soldier who came upon a beggar and shared his cloak with the beggar. In turn, the beggar revealed himself as the Christ. It has been told to me that his actions represent sharing . . . but not of everything, so that neither the giver nor recipient are lacking. His image is common in family-owned restaurants in New Mexico, and on many occasions, I have known those owners to feed persons in need.
Semana Santa	Holy Week
sheeps	more than one sheep. In English, "sheep" can be singular or plural. In Spanish the word for one sheep is "borrego." The plural form is "borregos." It is not uncommon to meet many older people who add an "s" at the end of "sheep."

Sierra Rota	Broken Mountain; in this book, a fictitious mountain
sobrino	nephew
Solo Vino	Comes Alone; could also be translated as "only wine"
talean	a dance
tío, tía	uncle, aunt
trastero	a cupboard where dishes or other items, usually culinary, are stored
vaca	cow; also spelled baca
vaquero	cowboy, a person who works with cows
valse	waltz
varas de San José	hollyhocks
la Varsovania	woman from Warsaw; a dance
vecino(s)	neighbor(s)
vega	meadow, pasture land
viejito(a)	old man, old woman, the diminutive; often as a term of endearment or respect
viga(s)	roof beam(s); usually exposed logs, overlaid with latillas
violinista	violinist

ABOUT THE AUTHOR

David Kyea has lived in Northern New Mexico for forty-eight years. He has worked as a ranch cook, woodcutter, ski lift operator, carpenter, shepherd, stockman, and adobe brick layer, cleared trails in the Pecos Wilderness, and planted trees at altitudes of ten thousand feet. His law enforcement career spanned twenty-six years as a Taos County Deputy Sheriff, District Attorney Investigator, Deputy Medical Investigator, and Union County Magistrate Judge. He is a graduate of the New Mexico Law Enforcement Academy and the FBI National Academy. He enjoys traditional New Mexico Spanish music and plays guitar, mandolin, tin whistle, violin, and viola. His writings have been published in the e-zine *Lunarosity* and by the New Mexico Book Coop in both *Voices of New Mexico* and *More Voices of New Mexico*. His first anthology, *KITE and Other Short Stories of New Mexico*, was published in 2020 and is available in print or as an e-book.

Spike   David   Nova